John Stone Outgunned!

A shot rang out, and the shotgun flew out of Stone's hands, making them sting. He turned to the right and saw a man lying on a hill, a rifle in his hands.

The hay moved in back of the wagon, and three men stood up, masks on their faces, rifles in their hands. . . .

SEARCHER

HELLFIRE

Josh Edwards

DIAMOND BOOKS, NEW YORK

HELLFIRE

A Diamond book / published by arrangement
with the author

PRINTING HISTORY
Diamond edition / August 1991

ISBN: 1-55773-554-9

Diamond Books are published by The Berkley Publishing
Group, 200 Madison Avenue, New York, New York 10016.
The name "Diamond" and its logo are trademarks
belonging to Charter Communications, Inc.

PRINTED IN THE UNITED STATES OF AMERICA

10 9 8 7 6 5 4 3 2 1

1

"THAR SHE IS!" shouted the stagecoach driver. "Clarksdale straight ahead!"

John Stone opened his eyes, and the stagecoach was shaking and jiggling through the warm New Mexico night. He was seated between a banker from California and a cavalry sergeant who reeked of cheap whiskey.

"I see it!" The banker peered out the darkened window. "We're almost there!"

Stone maneuvered past the sergeant and the lady seated opposite him, and stuck his head outside. The sage was pitch-black, but in the distance, lying in a valley, scattered lights flickered like a sprawl of diamonds. The horses' hooves pounded and the maniacal laughter of the stagecoach driver sailed out beneath the canopy of stars as he whipped the horses' tails.

Stone returned to his dust-covered seat. His legs were cramped from the long hours of sitting, and his toes were numb.

The banker, Edward McManus of San Francisco, puffed a cigar. He was in his fifties, with a thick gold chain hanging across his potbelly. Opposite Stone sat McManus's wife, Maureen, and Stone's knees had been touching hers throughout the trip. She was in her twenties, and had the look of a dance-hall girl.

Two other passengers were in the stagecoach. One was Slade, a tall cowboy in his forties who hadn't said much since

1

leaving Tucson. He looked out the window at Clarksdale, then pulled his head back into the stagecoach, his face expressionless in the dimness.

The other was a hardware salesman wearing a yellow suit and brown derby, who'd spent most of the trip describing his many wonderful products, and making foolish not-so-subtle advances toward Maureen McManus, who treated him with mocking condescension.

They'd been bounced and shaken by the constant movement of the stagecoach over uneven roads. None of them had bathed since leaving Tucson five days ago, which created a ripe atmosphere inside the coach. Cavalry Sergeant Bannon opened his eyes, burped, took out his flask, gulped some down, and screwed the lid back on.

"We're almost in Clarksdale," McManus told him.

Sergeant Bannon didn't reply; he closed his eyes and passed out again.

"Never saw a man consume so much whiskey," sighed McManus. "He hasn't seen a bit of the wonderful scenery we've passed on our trip. What a waste."

"Some people don't know what's good," replied Maureen McManus. "You could drop 'em in the middle of paradise, and they wouldn't know it."

Stone looked at the sergeant snoring softly in the dimness. The sergeant probably had seen enough scenery from atop his saddle to last him a lifetime.

"What are you going to do, Mr. Stone, after you arrive in Clarksdale?"

Stone turned to Maureen McManus, her green eyes just visible in the starlit darkness.

"Check into the nearest hotel and get some sleep."

"The best hotel in town," her husband boomed, "is the Carrington Arms right across from where they'll let us off. That's where we're staying. Perhaps we can have a drink together tonight?"

"I don't know the town," Stone replied.

"There's a saloon called the Emerald City, right on Main Street. We'll be there later, if you care to join us."

The hardware salesman, Donald Gershman, took out a little black book issued by his company and did his homework:

Clarksdale, New Mexico (pop. 2,768), is one hundred and fifty miles west of the Texas border. It is the major town in the region and has two hardware stores as of this printing. The center for the local ranching industry, and a way station for wagon trains on their way to Tucson, it will be on the route of the proposed Santa Fe–Abilene line of the T & R Railroad. A prosperous and growing community with a great future. All the comforts of the East in the middle of the wild frontier.

Sure, thought Gershman. *In a pig's ass.*

The horses strained at their harnesses as they ripped through the night. They saw the bright lights ahead and knew there'd be a big sweet-smelling barn with good grain and oats, and a dry place to sleep with all the other beasts that'd muscled their way across the world that day. As for their burdens in the coach, Maureen brushed her blond hair, the salesman smoothed his black mustache, McManus buttoned the top button of his pants, and Slade rolled a cigarette, his eyes cold as a reptile's.

Slade hadn't said much throughout the trip. He'd just sat and stared out the window, or slept. He looked like a man who'd been used roughly by the world, and now used it in the same way. McManus had tried to strike up a conversation on several occasions, but Slade hadn't responded.

The sergeant slouched in the corner. Stone had tried some Army talk with him, but the sergeant always backed away, maybe shy, maybe cynical, or maybe just another drunken trooper on a spree.

Stone checked his belongings, and his hands came to rest on his crisscrossed gunbelts. He wore two Colts in holsters slung low and tied to his legs. He touched the Colts with the palms of his hands, to make sure they were there. He could lose his wallet, he could lose his mind, but he didn't dare lose his Colts.

The night was lighter around the stagecoach, as it approached the edge of town, a jumble of wooden homes, one and two stories high. In the middle of the town was a long, wide, brightly lit street, and people walking around like ghosts in a dream, or so it seemed to travel-weary John Stone.

"Fifteen minutes after ten," McManus said, looking at the white face of his gold pocket watch.

"Hope the restaurants are still open," his wife replied. "I could use me a steak about now."

"I know just where to go," McManus replied. "Just leave it to me." He looked at Stone. "The Emerald City, the place I mentioned to you before, has the finest steaks in the world."

"I'll be there," Stone said; he was ready to gnaw on boot leather and saddlebags.

Maureen McManus's eyes twinkled in the darkness. Was she looking at him? The cavalry sergeant next to Stone sipped some liquid from his flask, preparing for his arrival. The salesman leaned toward Maureen McManus.

"I wonder if you'd mind if I joined you at the Emerald City?"

"It's a free country," she said in her faintly sarcastic tone. "You can go wherever you want."

The banker slapped him on the shoulder. "We'd love to see you. Just drop by."

Slade puffed his cigarette casually and looked out the window through small, flinty eyes. Stone read him as a man who'd slept under many open skies.

The stagecoach driver shouted happily atop his high seat, and the old Concord coach rumbled into Clarksdale. The passengers looked out the windows and saw rows of stores closed for the night, then a saloon that never closed, a restaurant, and a darkened barbershop with a painted pole.

Men swaggered on the sidewalks, pistol grips glinting in the moonlight. Some had just driven in from the sage, and others were dressed in eastern finery. A few women could be seen, wearing long gowns with bustles in back, the leading ladies in the town. Ordinary women were home sleeping, exhausted after a day of work tough enough to tire a mule.

And then there were the sporting ladies in the windows of the saloons. Stone knew a town like this would have lots of them. They came from all over America and all over the world, some brand-new, some worn-out, and all dreaming of the cattle king who'd carry them away.

The stagecoach hit the center of town, a crowd gathering as the driver pulled back the long wooden brake lever. A drunken cowboy opened the door.

"Where you folks from?" he asked, a crazy smile on his face.

"Tucson," replied the banker.

The cowboy leaned forward and grabbed the waist of Maureen McManus, lifting her out of the stagecoach and depositing her gently on the ground, and she smiled graciously all the way down. Slade was out the door next, and disappeared into the crowd. The cavalry sergeant climbed down and looked for the nearest saloon. Stone was next, stepping to the ground, and when he pulled himself erect he was taller than everybody in the crowd. He wore a red shirt with a black bandanna around his neck, and his faded blue jeans were tucked into the tops of his boots, cavalry style.

Across the street was the Carrington Hotel, lights gleaming from its downstairs windows. It was three stories high, the fanciest and most elaborate hotel Stone had seen in a long time. The sheets would be clean, the water hot, and if nobody tried to kill him in his bed, he'd get a night's sleep.

The stagecoach driver and his guard threw down the luggage. Stone snatched his saddlebags out of the air and pushed his way through the commotion, heading toward the Carrington.

It felt good to stretch his legs, and he climbed the steps leading to the veranda of the hotel, where a few men sat on rocking chairs, smoking cigars. They gave him the usual once-over, their eyes saying: *Who's this son of a bitch*? He entered the large lobby, and more people sat on plush furniture, while huge chandeliers provided light.

Stone approached the desk. "I'd like a room for the night."

The clerk had a long black mustache and a bald head. "How long are you staying, sir?"

"Until the next stage leaves for Santa Fe."

"That's tomorrow morning, sir."

"What time?"

"Nine in the morning. It only makes the run twice a month. The one tomorrow will be the last stage this month."

"I guess I'll just be staying one night," Stone said.

"A room for one night is fifteen dollars."

"That's a little over my head."

"It's our cheapest room, cowboy."

"Do you know of anything more reasonable in this town?"

"A lady named Mrs. Harder keeps a boardinghouse on the edge of town, and sometimes she has rooms for . . . travelers."

The clerk gave Stone directions to Mrs. Harder's establishment, and Stone slung his saddlebags over his shoulder, heading toward the door. Just then Edward McManus and his wife entered, followed by a retinue of drunken cowboys carrying their luggage.

"Couldn't find a room?" McManus asked Stone.

"Out of my price range."

Stone made his way down the main street of town, which was mostly a series of noisy saloons. A drink would be nice, but he ought to get settled first.

He came to the outskirts of town. It was dark and quiet, with no one about. The full moon shone golden in the sky, and the Milky Way blazed a path into the mountains in the distance.

The houses were darkened, made of wood. Some had fences and little gardens. The street was hard dirt covered with a film of dust.

No lights were on in Mrs. Harder's. Stone approached the door and knocked. He waited awhile and saw a light in one of the windows. The door opened. A little white-haired old lady with a face like a bird stood in front of him.

"What do you want?" she asked, sniffing him as if his character could be fathomed via her nostrils, and maybe it could.

"Room for the night," he said. "The clerk at the Carrington Arms sent me here."

"Two dollars."

"Can I get a bath?"

"Not till mornin', when we light up the stove."

She led him into the house. The rooms were small, furnished with sturdy chairs and tables, and a print of Gilbert Stuart's portrait of George Washington hung above the mantel. Opening a drawer in a hand-carved mahogany cabinet, she pulled out a key.

"Second floor at the end of the corridor." She looked him in the eye. "Now I want us to understand each other. This is a respectable home. I will tolerate no foolishness, unwarranted noise, rowdiness, or drunkenness. Mothers and young ladies stay here, and we tolerate no bad manners. Is that clear?"

"Yes, ma'am."

Stone climbed the stairs to the second floor. It was dark, the only light coming from the window at the end of the corridor.

He stopped to get his bearings, then found his door. The key wouldn't fit. He tried again, but it still wouldn't go.

A woman's voice on the other side of the door said: "I don't know who you are, but if you don't get away from my door I'm going to pull the trigger of this rifle I've got in my hand!"

Stone stepped quickly aside. "Sorry—wrong room."

He turned around and inserted the key into the opposite door. The key turned and Stone entered a small room with a bed, chair, and washstand. A Bible sat on the chair.

He closed the door and lit the lamp. Then he walked to the window and looked outside. He could see the glow of the downtown area over the rooftops of the houses in front of him. There was nothing he liked better than coming to a new town and looking around. Every town on the frontier was different in its own way, and you met the strangest people.

He hung the saddlebags from a bedpost and dropped onto a chair, wondering what to do next. He'd been sleepy before arriving at Mrs. Harder's boardinghouse, but the lady with the rifle next door had wakened him. Being threatened with death had that effect on a man. He wanted a drink, but needed a bath more, and he'd find someplace to soak in this town, he felt sure, even at this hour.

He decided to take his saddlebags with him, so he could change his clothes after he took the bath. But first he'd roll a cigarette.

He poured the makings out of his black leather tobacco pouch and rolled the cigarette. Smoothing the ends, he lit it with a match and leaned back in the chair. It's been a long trip, and he felt he'd spent it in a torture device. The wagon hadn't been designed for big men like himself.

He opened his shirt pocket and took out a photograph of a young blond woman in an isinglass frame. He looked at her for a few moments, then raised the frame and kissed her. He dropped the picture back into his pocket and buttoned the flap.

Getting up, he checked his gunbelts and pulled the saddlebags off the bedpost, draping them over his shoulder. He flung the door open, and simultaneously the door across the hall opened.

He found himself looking at a young woman wearing a high-necked blouse with peaked shoulders. Her eyes widened in fear at the sight of him.

"Don't shoot!" he said, raising his arms. Then slowly, he took off his old Confederate cavalry officer's hat. "I've got the room across the hall here. Was mixed up a few minutes ago, tried to get into your room by mistake. Name's John Stone. Do you know where I can take a bath at this time of night?"

Suspicion still in her eyes, she said: "Afraid not. Don't know much about this town. Just passing through."

"Where are you going?"

"Santa Fe."

"That's where I'm headed too. What's your name?"

"Priscilla Bellevue."

"If I can be of assistance, just let me know."

He peered past her and saw a chair identical to his, with an open Bible lying on the footstool in front of it. He tipped his hat and walked down the hallway to the stairs.

He heard her door close above him as he descended the stairs. He crossed the darkened parlor and left through the front door, stepping into the moonlight.

The glow of the downtown area drew him toward it like a moth to flame. He didn't know the names of the streets, he just followed the light. The closer he came, the more people he saw. Finally he reached the bright lights, and music, and the crowd of revelers.

Across the street was a saloon called the Shandon Star. He paused for a moment, then headed toward it, passing men having loud conversations, wagging their hands in the air. Pushing open the doors, he stepped inside. The bar was to the left, the chop counter to the right, and tables were scattered in between.

Stone walked up to the bar, finding an open spot between a cowboy passed out on his stool and a dude wearing a diamond stickpin in his tie.

"Whiskey."

The bartender poured the clear amber fluid into the glass. Stone picked it up and rolled some over his tongue, savoring the flavor. It was smoky as an old hickory fire and bright as the fields of grain that comprised its essence.

"I see you're wearing your old Confederate Army hat," said the dude next to Stone. "I guess you're one of them who never gave up."

"I gave up."

"Save all yer Confederate money, eh, feller? The South is a-gonna rise again, right?"

"The South will rise again," Stone said, "but Confederate money is nothing but wallpaper now."

The dude looked Stone up and down. "You a gamblin' man?"

"Depends on the game."

"I'm gettin' a game up later, with a few of my friends. You're welcome to join us."

John knew the dude was a professional cardsharp, with eyes like a ferret.

"First I've got to take a bath," Stone said. "You know where I can get one?"

"The Crystal Palace. It's a whorehouse, but you can get a bath and anything else you might want at the same time."

"Sounds like a pretty expensive bath."

"Everything good has a price."

"Can a man get a bath around here without the frills?"

"Sullivan's Tubs. No frills, but the water's hot and clean, and they give you a bar of soap. It's extra for the towel." He looked at Stone's holsters. "I don't understand how a man can buy Colts when there's Remingtons around." He reached under his coat and whipped out a Remington, holding it in the light of the lamps. "You see this strap of steel on top of this Remington? That gives it strength. Now look at one of your Colts. It don't have this strap of metal. The entire Colt is held together by two little wedges of metal at the bottom. That ain't enough."

"It's worked all right for me."

"But it's weaker—can't you see? It don't have this strap of metal on the top."

"I never had any trouble with it."

"Let me show you what I mean. Hand me yer gun, will you?"

Stone passed the Colt on his right to the gambler, who took it, turned it around, and pointed it at Stone, along with his Remington. Stone found himself looking down two gun barrels.

The gambler smiled. "You should never give yer gun to another man who you don't know."

"You're not going to do anything with it."

"What makes you so sure?"

"Gamblers don't want trouble with the law."

The gambler smiled as he handed Stone's gun back. "Usually I scare the shit out of people before I hand their guns back." He lifted his hat. "Glad to meet you. I'm Chance Stevens."

"John Stone."

"Let me buy you a drink."

"I was on my way to the tubs."

"They'll wait."

The bartender poured two more drinks, and Stone couldn't walk away from good whiskey. Chance Stevens raised his glass. "Happy days," he said.

Stone sipped the cool dusky liquid, and it tingled his palate. He felt himself settling down. The saloon was thick with smoke, and a waitress in a low-cut dress carried a tray of beer mugs past him.

"So you're an ex-Confederate officer down on yer luck." Chance Stevens sipped his own drink. "But you got sand in yer craw and you like a good drink of whiskey. That about it?"

"Just about."

"What do you do for money?"

"Odd jobs here and there."

"Just a drifter?"

"You might say that."

"There's a lot of money to be made in this country, for a man willing to stay in one place for a while."

"I intend to settle down first chance I get."

"What's stopping you?"

"I'm looking for somebody."

"Who?"

"A woman friend of mine."

"I was married a few times," Chance Stevens said. "It's a bad business. Cheaper to buy the milk than buy the cow."

Chance motioned to the bartender, who filled both glasses again. Chance raised his glass in the air. "To all the undefeated Galahads of the Noble Cause!"

He knocked his glass against Stone's, then tossed the whiskey down his throat, wiping his mouth with the back of his hand.

"You're obviously a gentleman," Chance said to Stone. "You don't look like one, but I can tell you're an educated boy. You sure sound like one. And here you are, just another frontier tramp, ain't that so?"

"What about you? A gambler's a drifter too."

"I'm not driftin' anymore," Chance said. "I'm stayin' right here in Clarksdale. There's too much money to be made. Everybody likes a good game of cards, and that's what I give 'em. Win, lose, or draw, it don't matter. The game is the only thing that counts."

Stone smiled. "Don't tell me you don't mind when you lose."

"Well, I might mind a little."

"I bet you mind a lot."

"You read me like a book, boy."

"Why don't *you* settle down, Chance? Get some land and cattle, instead of betting your life on a turn of a card."

Chance made a face as if he'd smelled something rank. "I don't want to walk ass deep in cowshit all day. There's nothin' in that for me." He pointed his forefinger to his head. "I'd rather make money with my mind. That's what gambling is. The real spirit of a man is in his mind, and that's the territory where I want to prove I'm the better man." He hooked his thumbs under the lapels of his expensive suit. "You think you're a smart feller, John Stone?"

"I get by."

"Let's lock horns—you and me. Come on back here after you take the bath. The stakes won't be high. I'll take it easy on you."

Stone downed the final drops of his whiskey. "Don't take it easy on me. I can take care of myself."

Stone headed toward the door, making his way through a mass of men drinking alcoholic beverages, their hats on the backs of their heads, laughing and talking, waving their arms in the air.

A woman in a red dress walked up to him. "Buy me a drink, cowboy?"

"I gotta take a bath."

"I'll take one with you." She smiled seductively.

"Sorry, but I'm engaged to get married."

"So'm I, but two grown-ups like us shouldn't worry about something as silly as *that*."

"If you're here when I get back, I'll buy you a drink."

He walked toward the door. The prostitute had been beautiful, a Scheherazade of the prairie. *And she could buy and sell me.*

Men in small groups were gathered in the street, holding glasses in their hands, having conversations. A buckboard rode past, and Stone saw the black collar of a preacher. Stone turned to the left and took a long stride, feeling something bump against his leg.

"Watch where you're goin'!" a man roared.

Stone turned around and saw a hunchbacked midget cowboy wearing a wide-brimmed hat with a high crown. "Sorry," Stone said.

The hunchback had on leather chaps with a red calico bandanna tied roughly around his neck. "Who the hell you think you are!" he said. "Just because you say you're sorry, you think that makes it all right, you son of a bitch!"

"I wasn't looking where I was going."

"Open yer goddamn eyes!"

Stone knew there was nothing he could say to please the man. All he could do was get away. He turned and stepped toward the street. Behind him he heard the slide of metal against greased leather.

"Hold it right thar, you son of a bitch!"

Stone stopped in his tracks.

"Turn around!"

Stone turned and saw the hunchback pointing his six-gun at him. The men who'd been in the street were fleeing toward alleys and doorways, or ducking down behind water troughs.

"You think you can push other people around," the hunchback said, "and just walk away afterward?"

"I didn't push you around."

"You saw me, but you thought you'd walk right fuckin' over me without me sayin' anythin', but you was wrong."

Stone looked at the gun in his hand. *Maybe I can get off a fast shot.* But the trouble with fast shots was they weren't accurate. Stone clicked his teeth and slowly raised his hands until they were level with the ivory grips of his pistols.

"Hold it right thar, or I'll blow yer damn head off!" the hunchback hollered.

Stone tensed his muscles. He towered above the hunchback in the shadows of the sidewalk, and men watched from their hiding places, or through the windows and open doors of the saloons.

"If you say I'm a liar," Stone said, "give me a chance to prove you're wrong."

"How you aim to do that?"

"Let Mr. Colt decide it."

The hunchback narrowed his eyes. He looked grotesque and weird standing there with a gun in his hand.

"You're not afraid, are you?" Stone chided him.

"Afraid of you!" the hunchback bellowed. "I ain't afraid of you! You ain't shit to me!"

"Let Mr. Colt decide it."

"He is gonna decide it."

The hunchback aimed down the barrel of his gun at Stone, and Stone thought, *I'd better make my play.*

A deep, strong voice rang out on the deserted street. "Drop that gun, cowboy, or you're a dead man!"

Stone saw a tall, silver-haired man in a long riding coat standing in the middle of the street, holding a gun in his right hand, pointing it at the hunchback.

"This is Sheriff Pat Butler talkin', and I got one of my deputies with me. We don't tolerate no gunplay in this town. You drop yer gun or I'm a-gonna kill you."

The hunchback let go of his gun. Out of the shadows came the deputy, carrying a rifle, and he picked the gun up. Sheriff Butler holstered his pistol and advanced from the street.

"What's yer name!" Sheriff Butler said to the hunchback.

"Dorchester."

"Mr. Dorchester, you're under arrest. The jail is thataway."

The sheriff pushed the hunchback, who sullenly walked away, looking down at the ground. He took several steps, then stopped and turned to Stone, his face corded with fury. "I'll see you again someday, and then there won't be no sheriff to save yer ass!"

Stone stared at the hunchback coldly. He wanted to remember that face and everything about the man, because next time he saw him it would be draw and fire.

Sheriff Butler and the hunchback continued down the street toward the jail. Stone loosed his bandanna and sat on a bench in front of a shuttered hardware store. He took out his tobacco and rolled a cigarette.

He'd thought the hunchback was going to kill him. The hunchback's finger had been tightening around the trigger. *I shouldn't've turned my back on him.*

The tubs were straight ahead. He arose, adjusted his gunbelt, and walked down the street toward the sign in the distance, illuminated by lanterns, that said:

SULLIVAN'S TUBS

He walked in the door. Before him in a large yard sat eighteen tubs, nine occupied by men washing themselves in the open air. Stone approached the man at the cash register.

"Number fourteen," the man said, hardly glancing up from his newspaper.

Stone walked back to number fourteen, an iron tub three feet high. A hatrack was next to it, and Stone took off his old Confederate cavalry hat, dusted it, and placed it next to a sleek new wide-brimmed cowboy hat. Then he unbuttoned his shirt.

The tubs were under the night sky, but the stove and fire was covered by a roof held up by wood posts. The man bathing himself next to Stone had a flask on a stool beside him, and his arm, covered with suds, arose from the tub and picked up the flask.

The man looked up at Stone. "Could you use a touch of real Irish whiskey?" He had a British accent and held the flask in the air.

Stone held out his hand. "If you don't mind."

The flask dropped into his hand, and Stone stared at it for a second. Then he unscrewed the lid. He'd been drinking rotgut since coming to the frontier, and hadn't drunk any real Irish whiskey for years.

He raised the flask to his mouth, paused a moment, and let some trickle in. It was smooth as silk, and he could taste its refinement. He let more trickle in, savored it, and swallowed it down.

"Mighty fine whiskey," Stone said, handing the flask back. "Where'd you get it?"

"Brought it with me from England, and there isn't much left."

"I'm grateful you shared it with me."

"You looked like a man who'd enjoy a fine glass of whiskey. By the way, my name's Dunwich."

"John Stone."

"What brings you to this town?"

"I'm on my way to Texas."

"What're you going to Texas for?"

"To see a friend of mine. What brings you here all the way from England?"

"In my opinion, the American frontier is the most exciting place in the world to be right now. Look around you: it's a land up for grabs, fortunes made and lost every day, people shooting each other constantly, men digging up hunks of gold from the ground, savages who'll skin you alive. The American frontier is inconceivable, and yet here it is, and you and I, my friend, are right in the middle of it. Another drink?"

Stone accepted the flask. Two burly Negroes approached, carrying a barrel of hot water on a stand. They wrestled the barrel off the stand and poured the water into the tub. Then one of them handed Stone a towel.

Vapors arose from the tub. Stone climbed in and sat down, his knees poking up through the steam. The hot water washed over him. He closed his eyes and relaxed.

"Where are you coming from?" Dunwich asked from the next tub.

"Arizona."

"Nice place?"

"If you like fighting Apaches."

"You sound as if you're talking from personal experience."

"I am."

"You've been attacked?"

"Yes."

"What was it like?"

"Everything you'd imagine, and worse."

Dunwich handed him the flask again. "Have a drink and tell me about it."

"The only thing you need to know is Indians hate white people and they're killers. I had a friend who was an Indian himself, and he told me to never trust an Indian."

"What happened to him?"

"He's dead."

"How'd he die?"

"You ask a lot of questions, Mr. Dunwich."

"Asking questions in my line of work. I work for the *Morning Sentinel*, a London newspaper, and you sound like an interesting fellow. Care for another drink? Tell me about the Indian who's dead."

"I'm a little tired."

"What are you doing when you leave here?"

"I'd planned to have dinner."

"Why not have dinner with me and my assistant, as our guest?"

"I never turn down a free meal."

"See you at the Emerald City in about an hour an a half."

Stone closed his eyes and relaxed against the back of the tub. The hot water reached like fingers into his joints and muscles and made them relax.

Arizona had been a bloodbath, thanks to the Apaches, but he found a man there who said he thought he'd seen Marie in Texas.

The man was dead now, Apaches had killed him, but when Stone showed him the picture of Marie, the man said she was a wife of a rancher in the San Antonio area.

Stone heard Dunwich arise from his tub and get dressed.

"Care for one last drink before I go?" Dunwich asked.

Dunwich was dapper in his carefully tailored suit of worsted wool. His cowboy hat looked dashing atop his head, and he wore new cowboy boots. Stone accepted the flask and sipped more Irish whiskey.

"Look forward to seeing you later," Dunwich said.

He walked away. Stone closed his eyes and relaxed in the hot water. A bird twittered on the roof of the shed that covered the stove. He drifted off into a reverie of Marie, dancing in the ballroom of her family's home, a slim-waisted woman with graceful hands. He felt a deep longing in his heart. *I'll find her in Texas.*

"What the hell d'ya think you're lookin' at!" a man thundered a few tubs from Stone.

"Just lookin' around," replied a second voice. "Don't do no harm to look around, does it?"

"You keep yer goddamn eyes off'n me!"

"Who the hell d'ya think yer talkin' to!"

"You know who I'm talkin' to!"

Stone heard a rush of water, a metallic click, a shot, and a gun was fired. The bullet whistled over Stone's head. Then a second bullet fired, and Stone heard a strangled cry.

"I'm hit!" a man said.

Stone raised his head above the wall of the tub and saw a stout hairy man fall to the ground. Standing over him was another man with a gun, a thin trail of smoke rising from the barrel, caught in a shaft of light from a coal-oil lamp.

"Everybody hold still," the man with the gun said. "I'm gittin' out of here, and if anybody tries to stop me, he's dead meat."

Stone measured the distance between himself and his guns, and they were too far away.

The man with the gun got dressed quickly, pulled on his boots, and ran off into the night. Stone moved the chair with his gunbelt closer to him. The men in the tubs resumed washing themselves. Just another late-night bath, as usual.

Stone sank into the warm water, letting it wash over his head, and it felt like baptism. A man lay dead on the ground nearby. *Went to heaven clean.*

Stone raised his head, lay back, and looked up at the sky. The smell of woodsmoke wafted past his nostrils, and someone was strumming a guitar. The tension and madness drained out of his body.

He gazed at Orion, the warrior in the sky, holding his sword in the cosmos ablaze with stars.

2

STONE WALKED TOWARD the Emerald City, carrying his saddlebags over his shoulder. He felt refreshed and clean in a green shirt with a black bandanna, and another pair of faded blue jeans.

His Confederate cavalry hat was square on his head and he was looking forward to a night on the town. There'd be some music, and maybe some dancing girls. He could see the bright lights of downtown Clarksdale in the distance, but around him was darkness, shuttered storefronts, a few drunks sleeping on benches.

He was aware of someone running toward him in the night. He was coming fast, straight at Stone, and Stone drew his guns.

Materializing out of the night was a young man with curly black hair, a mask of panic on his face. He had no weapons in his hands, but Stone held him in his sights as he passed by.

Stone had only seen him for a moment, but his face had said abject terror.

"Stop him!" somebody shouted. "He's a crook!"

The man with curly black hair disappeared into the darkness, and from the other direction a man with a mustache emerged, waving a six-gun, his face red with exertion.

He ran past Stone, and Stone followed him into an alley. They made their way to the backyard, and stood side by side, listening to the sound of hoofbeats.

"He's gittin' away!" the man said.

"What's he done?"

"Stoled my wallet out of my jacket while I was in the pisshouse. Took everythin' I got. Damned bastard must've follered me in, but I din't see him. I'm a-gonna git my horse and track the son of a bitch. I might not find him tonight, and I might not find him tomorrow, but I'll find him one day, and when I do . . ." He drew his finger across his throat. "What did you say yer name was?"

"John Stone."

"I'm Jesse Culpepper. Thanks for yer help."

Jesse Culpepper tipped his hat and ran off into the night. Stone walked back through the alley and headed toward the bright lights at the center of town.

He came to the front of the Emerald City, on a corner, surrounded by a wide veranda. Stone climbed the stairs to the veranda, where men and a few women sat on benches and chatted, sipping their favorite beverages in the golden light that spilled from the windows.

He passed through the doors, and inside was a plush sprawling saloon. A bar was on the left, another bar on the right, tables were in the middle, and the chop counter was in back, colored ladies working at the grill.

Stone's stomach was grumbling. He headed for the chop counter, making his way among tables crowded with men and women, and the air was thick with tobacco smoke.

"I say there—John Stone!"

Stone turned in the direction of the voice and saw Paul Dunwich arise from the sea of heads, waving his hand. At Dunwich's table was a brunette dressed in men's cowboy clothes that were far too big for her, and she wore a red bandanna around her neck.

"John, may I present my assistant, Diane Farlington."

Stone accepted her hand. They looked into each other's eyes.

"Paul's told me all about you," she said. "Please sit down and tell us about your experiences with Indians."

"Awfully hungry."

"I'll get the food," Dunwich said. "Have a seat. What would you like?"

"A steak well done with everything that comes with it."

Dunwich launched himself toward the chop counter, and Stone sat opposite Diane, removing his hat, placing it on an empty chair. His hair was dark blond, growing over his ears and down his back.

Diane looked at him. "So you're a real frontiersman, and you've actually known Indians. Tell me something about them."

"They'd shoot you as quickly as they'd shoot a rabbit. How long you been out here?"

"We've been west of the Mississippi about two weeks."

There was a bottle of whiskey in the middle of the table. She noticed Stone looking at it.

"Help yourself."

Stone took a glass, filled it half full of whiskey, and slugged it down.

"Paul told me you've fought Indians. What was that like?"

Stone refilled the glass and sipped whiskey off the top. She watched him intently, with bright shining eyes.

"You haven't answered my question," she said.

Stone drank the rest of the whiskey in the glass. Dunwich returned to the table carrying a platter covered with an immense steak, mashed potatoes, carrots, gravy, and a fat slice of bread. He placed it before Stone, and Stone reached for the silverware. He cut off a big chunk of steak and placed it in his mouth.

Diane watched as he chewed. She glanced at Paul, and he winked at her. Patiently they waited until Stone finished eating.

Stone looked around as he dined, reconnoitering the saloon. If anybody pulled a gun, he wanted to be the first one on the floor.

He pushed the plate away, drank some whiskey, and rolled a cigarette.

The two Britons watched him. "Where are you from?" Diane asked.

"South Carolina."

Paul took a notebook out of his shirt pocket and began writing. "Were you in the war?"

"Yes."

"What did you do?"

"Don't remember. It was so long ago."

"Come on now, Mr. Stone. You couldn't forget something like that."

"Afraid I have."

"We don't care about the war," Diane said. "Mostly we want to know about the Indians."

"Yes," said Paul. "Tell us about the Indians."

"If you want to know about Indians," Stone said, "you should go to Arizona. There are a lot of them around there."

"How long were you in Arizona."

"Around two months."

"In the bathhouse, you told me you'd actually known an Indian personally. What was he like?"

Stone reached for the bottle. "Indians are trained from infancy to be warriors. Killing is all they know."

"Have you ever killed somebody, Mr. Stone?" Diane asked.

Stone sipped his whiskey.

"Have I offended you?"

Stone finished the glass and poured another. "You don't know the territory," he said quietly.

"That's what we're talking with you for. So that you'll tell us what we need to know."

"All you need to know is this: If you're not careful, you won't live long. Everybody's buzzard food until proven otherwise."

"I believe you're trying to scare us."

"There are probably wanted killers in this room right now."

Diane smiled. "Really?"

Dunwich held up his hand. "Mr. Stone is right. The frontier is dangerous, and I'm fully prepared." He pulled back the right side of his impeccably tailored worsted suit and yanked out a Colt .44, which he pointed at Stone. "I'm capable of protecting myself and Diane, and furthermore, I know how to shoot."

Stone found himself looking down the barrel of a gun for the third time that evening. "Please point that thing someplace else."

"Don't worry. It's not loaded." Dunwich smiled, pointed it at the ceiling, and pulled the trigger.

The Colt discharged, sending a bullet into the rafters.

"My word," said Dunwich, an expression of astonishment on his face. "I didn't think it was loaded."

Everything in the saloon stopped. Dealers held their shuffles. Everyone looked in the direction of the shot, and every man moved his hand closer to his gun.

Dunwich saw everybody looking at him. "Terribly sorry. Just a mistake. Won't happen again."

He holstered his gun, sat down, and looked at Stone. "I almost killed you, didn't I?"

"You're a dangerous man," Stone replied.

Diane burst into laughter. "This is wonderful! *Englishman Shoots Notorious Western Gunman.* I can see the headline in the *Morning Sentinel.* And it'd be an authentic story because here I am, your faithful reporter, right in the middle of it."

"I can see a different headline," Stone replied. "*Englishman Hanged on American Frontier.* How do you like that one?"

"Not bad."

Dunwich smiled with embarrassment. "I suppose I should be more careful with this gun. Actually, I've never fired it before."

Stone stared at him. "You're in an enclosed space with armed men, most of them with violent natures, and you're carrying a gun that you've never even fired?"

"That is correct," Dunwich said. "It just hasn't seemed that dangerous to me."

"I've been here over four years, and I know what I'm talking about. You'd better start being more careful, otherwise you might find yourself in deep trouble very suddenly, and you won't have a chance."

Dunwich looked around him. The cowboys were easing back to whatever they'd been doing before he'd fired his six-gun. "I didn't realize," he said, "that it was so dangerous here. Nothing bad has happened yet."

"Let me tell you what I've gone through tonight," Stone said. "Right after I came to town a man in a bar pointed two loaded pistols at point-blank range at me and smiled. Then, out on the street, I nearly got shot in the back. After that I nearly got shot by mistake while I was taking a bath. Then I was witness to a robbery. Just now I was nearly shot through the head by you. And I only arrived a few hours ago."

"Sounds like you've had a rather interesting night. Are you getting all of this down, Diane?"

"Every word of it," Diane replied, smiling as she wrote in her notepad.

"I still don't think you understand," Stone said to her. "You've got to exercise prudent caution. Otherwise you're simply not going to survive."

"Don't worry about me," Diane said. "I can take care of myself." She reached into her shirt pocket and pulled out a derringer, pointing it at Stone.

"I hope that's not loaded," he said.

She looked him in the eye, and a faint smile came over her face. "It is."

"Please point it in another direction."

Stone looked into her eyes, and she didn't flinch. Her face was serious, even solemn. Then she smiled and dropped the derringer back into her shirt pocket.

"Had you scared for a moment, didn't I?"

"I thought you might shoot me, yes."

"I'll do anything to get a good story, Mr. Stone, but I wouldn't go *that* far."

Dunwich placed his hand on Stone's shoulder. "Let me make a proposition to you. I'll give you twenty American dollars, in gold, if you'll give us two days of your time. We'll put you up in the best hotel in town, we'll eat in the finest restaurants, drink the best whiskey, and you'll tell us about all your adventures, for the *Morning Sentinel*. I happen to know that cowboys in this region earn thirty American dollars a month, so this is a most generous offer, as I'm sure you realize. What do you say?"

"Sorry," Stone said. "I'm leaving tomorrow morning on the stage to Santa Fe."

"Why are you going to Santa Fe?"

"Personal."

Diane's eyes brightened. "We can go with you, and you can tell us your story on the road. Sounds like it might be fun. Will we have to worry about Indians?"

"I believe there are Comanches and Kiowas in the area."

"How thrilling!"

"And you always have to watch out for road agents."

"Ah, the dashing road agents."

Stone groaned. There was no use trying to reason with them. Their brains were addled.

He heard a voice behind him. "If it ain't the undefeated Galahad of the Noble Cause."

Stone turned around and saw Chance Stevens, the gambler.

"I've been looking for you," Chance said. "Mind if I sit down?"

Dunwich replied: "By all means."

Chance sat at the table and looked more closely at Lady Diane. "By God, it's a woman!"

Lady Diane laughed delightedly and Chance turned back to Stone. "Care to cut cards?"

"I'm a little busy right now."

Chance looked at the bottle. "Mind if I take a drink?"

Dunwich said: "Go right ahead."

Chance poured himself a glass, and the two Britishers stared at him.

"Are you a professional gambler?" Dunwich asked pleasantly.

"That's right." Chance grinned. "Care to cut a game of cards?"

"What do you play?"

"Anything you like."

"I'd like to learn how to play poker."

"I'm a professional gambler, not a teacher. I play for money."

Dunwich took out a handful of gold coins and dropped them on the table. "I have money."

Chance stared at the coins, glinting in the dim light. "I don't think it'd be fair for me to play with somebody who don't know the game."

"Chance really doesn't care about the money," Stone explained. "He mainly gambles for the intellectual challenge."

Dunwich looked at Chance. "Is that true?"

"I do it for both."

"I'm a fast learner," said Dunwich, "and I like intellectual challenges. Let's play a few hands."

Chance reached into his pocket and took out a deck of cards. "Care to deal?" he asked Dunwich.

"I told you I don't know how to play poker. However, if you can explain the rules, I'd be happy to try."

"Well," said Chance, "the easiest kind of poker to play is

draw poker." He explained the rules, what beat what, and how to draw. Then he shuffled and cut the deck, handing it to Dunwich.

"Cut it again," he said.

Dunwich cut the deck and threw one card to Chance. "Are you in?" he said to Stone.

"No thanks," said Stone, seeing the gleam in Dunwich's eyes. This English dandy was fast by nature, and there was something clever in his style. *Let Chance handle him.*

Dunwich dealt himself a card, then threw another one to Chance. Diane stared at Chance as though he were a genie who just popped out of a bottle. "Is that a real diamond stickpin?" she asked.

"Yes, ma'am."

"Nice touch. You know, you're really put together very well. I especially like the black hat. Makes you look evil."

"I am evil."

"In what way?"

Chance studied his hand. It consisted of a king, a jack, two nines, and a tray.

"Care to open?" Dunwich said, a sporting twinkle in his eyes, as if he'd just spotted the fox.

Chance threw a fifty-cent piece on the table, and so did Dunwich. Stone pushed back his chair.

"Where are you going?" asked Diane.

"To the bar."

"Don't go far," Chance said to Stone. "You and I've got a game to play."

Stone walked to the bar, and Diane followed him. They passed tables surrounded by gamblers, and heard a steady roar of conversation punctuated occasionally by a shout. Stone spotted Slade, the cowboy from the stagecoach, seated alone at a table against the wall, sipping a glass of whiskey. Their eyes met, but they didn't smile or wave.

Stone and Diane came to the bar. Stone leaned over the rail, and Diane imitated him.

"I'm having such a good time," she said. "This is *so* much better than London."

"What did you do in London?"

"Mostly I went to parties, and they were usually boring."

"Are you royalty by any chance?"

She looked startled. "How did you know?"

"Just a guess."

"I'm Lady Diane Farlington, and Paul is the Earl of Dunwich. We're here on a lark."

"Every man in this room is carrying at least one gun, and you think you're on a lark?"

"I think they're charming. I don't bother them and they don't bother me. We understand each other."

"What's yer poison?" the bartender said, and he wore a patch over one eye.

"Whiskey," Stone replied, and he turned to Diane. "How about you?"

"The same."

The bartender stared at her with his one good eye. "Are you a man or are you a woman?"

"A woman."

"What the hell you wearin' that getup fer?"

"I thought it looked rather nice."

"A woman should look like a woman, not a man."

"This is a new country, and we must dress accordingly."

"You should wear a dress." The bartender poured two glasses of whiskey, and Stone paid him.

She grasped her glass firmly. "Let's drink to our new collaboration."

"What collaboration?"

"You're going to tell Paul and me all about your fascinating adventures."

"I'm afraid I'm leaving first thing in the morning."

"I know. The stage to Santa Fe. We're going with you. And you're going to tell us everything."

"You can take that stagecoach if you want, but I'm not going to tell you anything."

"Why not?"

"My life is nobody's business but mine."

"You don't look very prosperous. Couldn't you use the money? Tell me about your Indian friend."

"Don't want to talk about him."

"Why?"

"Personal."

"Where did you meet him?"

"Hello, cowboy," said the voice of a woman.

Stone looked in the direction of the voice and saw the whore with the red dress whom he'd run into on the street earlier in the evening.

"You said you'd buy me a drink later," she said. "Remember?"

"What did you say your name was?"

"I didn't say, but it's Naomi."

"May I present Diane Farlington, from London."

Naomi looked around. "Where?"

Stone indicated Lady Diane. "Right here."

"I thought that was a man."

"I'm no man," Lady Diane said.

"Why do you dress like one?"

"These are the best clothes when you're riding the range."

"Have you ever ridden the range?"

"I intend to soon."

"Do you know how to ride a horse?"

"Of course. Do you?"

"I was born on a horse."

Stone turned to the bartender. "A drink for the lady."

"Name yer poison," the bartender said.

"Whiskey," said Naomi, gazing with distaste at Lady Diane. "She yer woman?"

"I'm nobody's woman," Lady Diane replied.

"I'm not surprised, seein' how you dress."

Stone heard a booming male voice behind him. "Harlot of Babylon!"

Everybody turned and saw a man wearing a white clerical collar with a black suit and a black hat. He pointed his finger at Naomi and hollered:

> *"The daughters of Zion are haughty,*
> *and walk with stretched-forth necks*
> *And wanton eyes*
> *Walking and mincing as they go,*
> *and making a tinkling with their feet;*
> *Therefore the Lord will smite them with a scab*
> *And the Lord will lay bare their secret parts."*

Naomi raised her glass of whiskey. "He follows me everywhere. I wish he'd leave me alone."

"Harlot of Babylon!" the preacher continued. "Repent while you still have time!"

"Tomorrow," Naomi said.

"There may not be a tomorrow for you, harlot!"

Naomi pulled a .22 caliber Smith & Wesson First Model 1857 Revolver out of her red satin pocketbook. "There may not be a tomorrow for you either, preacher man."

"You can shoot me, but you can't shoot Jesus."

Stone stepped between them. "Let me buy you a drink," he said to the preacher.

"I won't drink at the same bar as that harlot."

"Drink over here with me."

"Whiskey!" said the preacher.

The bartender filled a glass for the preacher, who drained it dry in one gulp. He slammed the glass on the bar and looked at Naomi. "Young lady, you need a good horsewhipping!"

Naomi sidled next to Stone. "I have a room not far from here."

"I told you I'm engaged to be married."

"You should have your last fling, while you've got the chance."

Diane moved closer to them, still writing. "I say there, Stone—is she propositioning you?"

"Yes."

"How much do you charge?" Diane asked Naomi.

"Five dollars . . . for you."

"I wasn't asking for me. I was asking for him."

"Why are you asking for him?"

"She's writing an article for a British newspaper," Stone explained.

The preacher shouted:

> *"Though your sins be as scarlet*
> *they shall be white as snow;*
> *Though they be red like crimson*
> *They shall be as wool!"*

"I can't git rid of him," Naomi said. "He wants to save my honor . . . for himself."

"I want to save you for Jesus!" the preacher raved.

Chance Stevens stepped toward them, an expression of profound disbelief on his face. "He cleaned me out," he said to Stone. "All I got left is this." He held a coin up in the air. "Bartender, a whiskey if you don't mind—and fast!"

Dunwich followed him to the bar. "No hard feelings, I hope."

"Whipped me in my own town," Chance said to Stone. "He comes at the cards in a queer way." Chance looked like a man who just stepped on a rake and got it in the face. The bartender poured him a drink, and he guzzled it down. "Flat broke on my ass again. Everything happens to me."

"If you like," Dunwich said, "I can give you some back."

Chance looked at Stone. "Did you hear that? Now he's insulting me."

"I didn't mean to insult you, old boy. How much do you need? It's only a game, you know. Take it all—I don't care."

Dunwich placed a pile of coins on the bar, and everybody stared at it. It was twenty or thirty dollars at least, and a cowboy had to work sixteen hours a day for a month to earn that much money.

"Go ahead, take it," Dunwich said.

Chance whipped out his Remington and pointed it at Dunwich. "I ought to kill you."

Stone felt that characteristic moment surging—the crazy cowboy temper, the readiness to fight to the death over nothing. And Dunwich, the fool, thought he was dealing with an English gentleman.

"All we did was play a game of cards."

"You said you never played poker before."

"I'm a fast learner."

"Nobody learns that fast."

"I'll give your money back, if that's the way you feel about it."

"It's not the money. I don't like to be cheated."

"I'm not accustomed to being called a cheat."

"Well, how's about fourflusher? You tricked me into playin' you, and then you cheated me. You lied when you told me you never played poker. You play poker like you been playin' it all your life."

Dunwich stared at the gun in his hand. "I've never cheated anybody. You've insulted me, sir, but it's not worth either of us dying for. Will bare-knuckle combat satisfy you?"

Chance thought for a few moments, then holstered his Remington. "You're on."

Dunwich and Chance walked toward the doors of the saloon. A crowd followed, Stone and Diane among them.

Diane reached for Stone's arm. "Why doesn't somebody stop them?"

"Fights break the monotony, and some are very entertaining."

"Somebody can get hurt."

"That's what makes them entertaining."

Dunwich and Chance walked into the middle of the street and faced off. The crowd made a circle around them, drunks pushing their way toward the front, spilling drinks on other people. Several arguments ensued, while others took bets on who'd win. The odds were up to five to one for Chance, who was a known quantity of deadliness, the Englishman was anybody's guess.

"Why don't you go for the sheriff?" Diane said to Stone.

"If he's around, he'll come."

"Why doesn't somebody do something? This isn't just going to happen, is it?"

"Yes."

"I really think you should do something, Mr. Stone."

"What?"

"Get out in the middle of the street and stop them."

"Why?"

"It's wrong to fight."

"Says who?"

"Me!"

She walked resolutely into the middle of the street, chest out, swinging her fists back and forth smartly, as if she were going to war. A smile spread over Stone's tanned features. The entertainment had arrived.

She walked in between the two combatants, who were rolling up their sleeves, and held out both her hands. "Gentlemen," she said, "you're not going to do this."

Dunwich lay his jacket on her outstretched arm. "Hold this for me, Diane dear, will you?"

"Paul, you're making a fool of yourself."

"A woman couldn't understand these things. Please step

back." He raised his fists and danced lightly on his toes.

"You're supposed to be reporting the news, not making it."

"Out of the way," Dunwich said. "Stand clear. That's a good girl."

She refused to move. "Stop being an idiot, Paul! This isn't fun anymore!"

"Will somebody please move Lady Diane out of the way."

Two drunken cowboys detached themselves from the crowd and grabbed her arms and legs, sweeping her off her feet. Her hat fell off and her brown curls tumbled out, dragging in the muck.

"Now see here!" she said, squirming, trying to break loose.

They dropped her into the muck, and she landed with a splat. Getting up, spitting a grain of dirt out of her mouth, she turned around and saw the Earl of Dunwich and Chance Stevens go at each other.

Chance threw the first punch, a tentative jab, and Dunwich danced to the side on the balls of his feet. He was always in motion, like a jumping jack bouncing around, his legs slightly bent and knees sticking out to the sides.

Suddenly he darted in and shot his right fist forward. It slammed into Chance's face, and Chance counterpunched but Dunwich was gone.

Chance's lip had burst when caught between his teeth and Dunwich's hard knuckles. Blood dripped down his chin, onto his black goatee. He looked at Dunwich bouncing up and down in front of him, cried out, and charged.

Dunwich danced to the side at the last moment while delivering a sharp punch to the side of Chance's head. Chance tripped and fell into the mud, shook his head, and quickly jumped to his feet again, raising his fists and moving them in circles.

Dunwich bounded around the ring, his face steely. Suddenly he charged again, but this time Chance was waiting for him. Both men swung at the same moment, and both went down.

Each lay on the ground in the middle of the street, struggling to get up. Diane ran to Dunwich.

"Are you all right!"

Cobwebs were in his head, and he tried to stand. Then he heard a deep booming voice.

"What's goin' on here?"

Everybody turned in the direction of the voice, and saw Sheriff Pat Butler standing there, light from the Last Post Saloon gleaming behind him.

Dunwich got to his feet, a sheepish look on his face. Chance snarled as he rose from the ground, mud all over him.

"We don't allow fightin' in this town. Clear the street."

Dunwich and Chance looked at each other. The crowd broke up and streamed into saloons. Diane looked at Dunwich's bruised features. "Are you hurt?"

"Nothing like some good fisticuffs to sharpen a man's senses."

"I thought he was going to shoot you."

"So did I."

"How did you beat him at cards?"

"Beginner's luck, I guess." Dunwich raised his hand in the air and shouted: "A round of drinks on me!"

The crowd followed them into the Emerald City Saloon, leaving Chance in the middle of the street, covered with mud, a defiant frown on his face.

He smacked his hat against his leg, to shake the dirt out, and put it on his head, then skulked into an alley, his hands in his pockets, grumbling revenge.

Meanwhile, the crowd gathered around the bar, and the bartender set up the glasses. Dunwich's arm was around Lady Diane's shoulders. "What a grand time!" he said.

She felt her mood improving. Nobody had gotten hurt, and she still was having her great adventure on the American frontier. "Yippee!" she shouted.

Stone observed them from the other end of the bar. He'd seen it happen before. People who behaved normally all their lives went berserk on the frontier.

The piano started playing. Waitresses carried trays of whiskey around the room. Stone looked at the clock above the bar. It was nearly midnight. He'd have one last drink and go home.

Dunwich raised his glass in the air. "To America!" he shouted.

Everyone cheered and tossed down the whiskey. Stone was one of them, and it burned his gizzard. He coughed, spat into the cuspidor, and rolled a cigarette.

"Mr. Stone?"

Stone turned and saw Edward McManus, the banker from San Francisco, twirling his mustache. "Care to join us?"

Stone looked in the direction of the banker's gaze, and saw a large round table surrounded by well-dressed men and women, with three bottles of whiskey upon it.

He followed McManus to the table, and the only two empty seats were on either side of Maureen McManus. Stone sat to her right, and McManus to her left.

"Captain John Stone," McManus said, making the introduction. "He arrived with us on the stagecoach. Used to be a Confederate officer, and now he's looking for a woman, isn't that right, Captain?"

Stone reached for the bottle closest to him and filled a glass. He poured the fine bourbon down his throat and it brought a faint blush to his cheeks. He was drunker then he'd been in a long time. Then he lit his cigarette.

"Where have you been?" Maureen McManus asked.

"Checked into a hotel and had a bath."

"You smell divine, and you look so much better now that you've shaved."

Stone poured himself another glass and drank it down.

McManus leaned forward, so he could see Stone better. "How do you like Clarksdale?"

"They've got a good sheriff."

A new voice joined the conversation. "Damn right we have. I'm Judd MacIntosh, the mayor of Clarksdale. Glad to make your acquaintance."

Stone shook hands with the distinguished-looking gentleman in the dark suit and striped vest, who was wearing a derby.

"This is a law-abiding town," the mayor said. "That's why it's a good investment. If you have any money to invest, Captain Stone, this is the place to do it. Clarksdale'll be as big as San Francisco someday!"

"I'll drink to that," Stone said.

Mayor MacIntosh continued to trumpet the economic attractions of Clarksdale. "The railroad'll be here within two years," he said. "By then the town'll be five times what it is today, and another year after that we expect it'll triple in size."

"I'll drink to that."

"I was speaking to a group of French investors just the other day. They said they'd rather put their money here than in the Suez Canal. I tell you, the man who invests a dollar here in Clarksdale today will have twenty dollars to show for it in five years."

"I'll drink to that."

The mayor's voice droned on, and Stone closed his eyes. The tumult around him became a steady roar that sounded like the hoofbeats of cavalry charging across a plain. He saw himself atop his horse, his saber in his hand, leading old Troop C into the fray. Yankee bullets whizzed over his head, and cannonballs plowed through the ranks of his men as they thundered into the maw of hell.

He felt a hand drop into his lap underneath the table. Opening his eyes, he turned to Maureen McManus. Her eyes were bleary and she teetered from side to side.

"Have you ever been to San Francisco?" she asked.

"No."

"If you ever visit, you must look us up. We'd love to have you as our guest, wouldn't we, Edward?"

"Indeed, my dear."

"Time for me to go," Stone told them, arising from the table.

McManus said: "So soon?"

"Have to catch a stagecoach in the morning."

"So do we. Who needs sleep?"

Everyone at the table laughed. Stone felt dizzy as he made his way to the bar. A man shouldn't get drunk among strangers. He lurched alongside the bar, passing cowboys, freighters, dudes, and ladies of the night.

An arm reached out to him. "Captain Stone!" The Earl of Dunwich stood at the bar beside Lady Diane Farlington. "Where are you going, Captain Stone? Let me buy you a drink!"

"I shouldn't . . ."

"Of course you should."

Stone saw a glass of whiskey suspended in the air in front of him. He took it out of Dunwich's hand and carried it to his lips, a few drops spilling onto his shirt. He sipped half the glass down.

"It's decided," Diane said. "We're going on that stagecoach

with you tomorrow and we'll telegraph your story to the Sentinel's offices in New York from the next town."

Stone was about to tell her she'd get no story from him, then recalled the twenty dollars they'd promised him. He became confused, and thought his mind might clear if he took another drink. Raising the glass to his mouth, he became aware that the Emerald City had become very quiet.

He looked up and saw Sheriff Pat Butler striding across the room, followed by two of his deputies, and they looked like hard men. Butler wore his long canvas riding coat and his hat low over his eyes, shading his face from the lamplights.

"I heard some dumb galoot shot a bullet through the roof in here a while ago!" Sheriff Butler shouted. "Who is he?"

Everyone looked at Dunwich, who stepped forward, a smile on his face. "I say, Sheriff—I'm afraid that was me. Sorry. I didn't know the gun was loaded."

"Hand it over."

"Beg your pardon?"

"You're under arrest for shootin' yer iron in a public place. Hand it over or I'll kill you where you stand."

Dunwich could feel the tension in the air. The sheriff and his deputies were poised in front of him, their hands near their guns.

"Sheriff, I think you should know that I'm the Earl of . . ."

They drew their guns, and he raised his hands into the air.

"Git his iron, Tony," said the sheriff.

Tony, a lean whiplash of a man, approached Dunwich, searched him, and found the gun in its holster beneath Dunwich's muddied suit. He drew the gun and stuffed it into his belt.

"Get goin'," Tony said.

"Where?"

"The jail."

"The jail!"

Tony pushed Dunwich, who stumbled toward Sheriff Butler.

"I say there, Sheriff," Dunwich said, "do you think I could possibly have a talk with the magistrate?"

Sheriff Butler laughed and pushed him toward the door. Diane ran after them. "Sheriff—could I please have a word with you!"

The Sheriff stopped and turned around, looking at her disapprovingly. "You must be his wife."

"Not exactly," Diane said, pulling a muddy hair away from her eye, "actually we're just friends, and he's a good man, not a troublemaker or a danger to anyone. He didn't mean to shoot his gun. It was only an accident. No one was hurt. Can't you be reasonable?"

"I ain't reasonable, ma'am. I'm the sheriff and the law is the law."

Sheriff Butler walked off, following Dunwich on his way to the door.

Diane ran after them and caught up with Dunwich.

"Don't worry, Paul," she said. "I'll start looking for a solicitor immediately. Be sure to take notes all the time you're in jail. We'll wire them to London first thing in the morning."

Dunwich looked toward the sheriff. "Are there clean sheets in the cell?"

"Clean boards," Sheriff Butler replied with a grin. "Soft too."

"Nothing bad ever happens to a reporter, darling," called Diane. "It's all material."

They marched off to jail. Diane felt a hand on her shoulder. John Stone stood there, reeling drunk. "The district judge'll come to town and there'll be a trial," he said thickly. "Dunwich'll pay a fine and go free. Nothing to worry about." Stone burped as he raised his Confederate cavalry hat from his head. "Good night."

He staggered toward the door. Around him, the crowd had gone back to their card games and bottles of whiskey. Somebody screamed in a dark corner. The piano began to play. Stone pushed open the doors and stepped onto the sidewalk.

The cool night air hit him, and he smelled the piquant fragrance of the sage. His head and limbs felt heavy, and the street spun for a few seconds. He took off his hat, running his fingers through his thick hair.

He got his bearings, then put his hat back on. Taking out his bag of tobacco, he rolled a crooked cigarette, spilling half the tobacco into the street. Licking the gummed paper, he reached for his matches and found they weren't there. He was out.

He careened toward the nearest group of men and stuck his cigarette amid them. "Anybody got a light?"

A flame appeared in front of him. Stone sucked the cigarette and its end began to burn.

He stumbled away, heading toward his rooming house, hearing the music behind him.

"Going somewhere without me?" asked a female voice behind him.

He turned around, and it was Naomi in her red dress, her long gold earrings glittering in the light of the moon.

"Goin' home," Stone said heavily. "Got to get up early."

"Why don't you come home with me? I'll take good care of you."

He stared at her through bloodshot eyes. "I'm engaged to be married. I've told you before, but somehow you won't listen. I'm in love with another woman, and I'm not interested in anybody else."

"No?" she asked, unbuttoning her bodice.

Stone stared transfixed at her magnificent orbs.

"Still not interested?" she asked.

"Can't." He raised his hat and burped. "Good night."

He turned and walked away. She followed, buttoning her bodice quickly, and caught up with him.

"You're a strange man," she said. "What's wrong with you? Don't you feel what other men feel?"

"I feel it for one woman, and I'm on my way to see her now."

"You should never throw away a good time, because life is hard, and good times are few and far between."

He turned and faced her, his eyes aglow. "A man has to stand for something."

"What do you stand for?"

He puffed his cigarette and tottered in the middle of the street. "I . . . hardly know anymore." He lifted his hat. "Nothing personal. You're a beautiful woman, and I'm drunk as the lord."

"You're a fool."

He shuffled down, hitched up his gunbelts, and made his way down the street toward his rooming house. She watched him go, then turned and walked back to the Emerald City Saloon.

Stone turned onto a dark street, seeing pinwheels of light in front of him. Stars pulsated in the sky. He felt dizzy, and wished he had a drink.

He heard something move in the darkness on the sidewalk to his right. He was in the middle of the street and turned toward it, drawing both his guns.

He swallowed hard, realizing he was sloshed in the middle of a dark deserted street. Somebody could shoot him, take his money, and run away. He reeled toward the shadows, pointing his guns before him.

He heard the sound again. Peering ahead through the darkness, he saw a man passed out on a bench twenty yards away. The man moaned softly, and Stone looked down at him.

He wasn't much older than Stone, and in his hand was an empty bottle of whiskey. *If I'm not careful, I'll end up this way*, Stone said to himself.

He holstered his guns and stumbled down the street to the rooming house. It was dark, with no lights in any windows, and the moon bathed the scene in the spectral glow. His eyes were heavy and every step was an effort.

He stopped in front of the rooming house, aware of a weight in the back of his pants. Reaching around, he felt the Earl of Dunwich's metal flask in his back pocket. *How the hell did that get there?*

He pulled it out of his back pocket and shook it. *Can't let fine Irish whiskey go to waste*.

Unscrewing the top, he brought the mouth of the flask to his lips. The shimmering liquid trickled down his throat and warmed his stomach. He drained the flask dry, screwed the lid back on, and stuffed it into his back pocket again.

He staggered toward the front door and opened it silently, entering the rooming house. It was quiet, filled with fragrant cooking odors mixed with the smells of soap and the flowers in the vase on the kitchen table.

He tiptoed toward the stairs, the floorboards, creaking beneath his boots. His hat was crooked on his head and his shirt half untucked. He climbed the stairs, and suddenly became aware that he didn't have his saddlebags with him.

Where the hell are they? he wondered. A wave of dizziness passed over him. All the whiskey he'd drunk, the food he'd eaten, the lack of sleep and hardships of two weeks in a stagecoach combined and hit him at the same moment. He swayed, reaching for the banister, but missed and lost his footing. With a low growl he went tumbling down the stairs, banging his head against the post at the bottom.

He lay sprawled on his back, his chest rising and falling with his respiration.

"What in the name of heaven and hell is going on out there!" a woman screeched.

Stone saw his landlady standing above him in a nightdress, her white hair covered by a tasseled sleeping cap, and she was wielding a broom.

"I told you there'd be no drunkenness in this house! Get out of here this instant!"

He tried to get up, and she kicked him in his hindquarters. He fell on his face and she kicked him again. Then she started beating him with the broom.

Stone struggled to rise. The room spun around and blows rained upon him. He grabbed the edge of a tablecloth in an effort to right himself, and a vase crashed to the floor.

"Out!" she hollered. "I'll have no drunken pigs in my home!"

Stone lunged toward the door, aimed for the knob, and missed it. Again he lost his footing and again crashed to the floor. The old lady slammed him on the back with the broom. He grabbed the doorknob and twisted it, diving onto the porch, tumbling over, and falling down the stairs.

He lay at the bottom of the stairs on his back and looked up at the landlady standing on the porch brandishing her broom. "You get away from here, you damned rum pot, and don't never come back again!"

Stone staggered down the street, his old Confederate cavalry hat askew on his head. He felt sick and dizzy, as if he was going to faint.

"I've got to lie down," he muttered. "I think I'm going to die."

He didn't dare lie down in the street, and he had to get away from private property. Wheeling, he saw mountains in the distance, outlined in silver by the light of the moon.

He headed for the mountains, bent forward, tripping over his own feet, uncoordinated, stumbling, gasping for air. His mind was fogged and all he knew was he had to find a quiet place to lie down.

He came to the edge of town, and before him stretched the sage, with the mountains in the distance like a massive length of weird calligraphy. He charged onto it like an old buffalo about to die.

The wind blew across the sage, and a tumbleweed danced by on its endless journey. Stone tripped on a rock, righted himself, and plunged onward. He smelled the wild fragrance of the endless prairies, and saw the stars ablaze above him. The air was cool and felt like water rushing against his face; he took deep draughts of it and hollered like a moose.

He reached above the tried to touch a star, but it eluded him. His foot caught on a dead branch and he dropped to the ground, rolling over, landing on his back.

The ground beneath him was level and devoid of rocks. He closed his eyes and fell asleep in a little gully, beneath the stars.

3

THE SUN SEARED his eyeballs, and he awoke. He was huddled with his back against the wall of the gully, out of the path of the wind. It had grown cold at night, and he'd had no blanket. He felt frozen to the core of his bones.

The sun had risen over the peaks of the mountains, showering its bright rays upon the sage, and Stone remembered he had a stagecoach to catch. He raised himself to a sitting position, drew his guns, and shook the sand off them. Testing the mechanisms, determining the guns were in working condition, he holstered them and stood.

He couldn't see the town from the bottom of the gully. The sage stretched forth endlessly before him, and a prairie dog ran by, stopped to look at him curiously, and then continued running.

Stone climbed out of the gully and saw the town asleep in the dawn light. To his left was a small meandering stream fifty yards away.

He checked his pockets and found his money, but there wasn't much left. The picture of Marie was in his shirt pocket; he didn't have the courage to look at her. He'd lost his saddle-bags with all his clothes. He had a hangover. It was going to be a bad day.

He came to the stream, dropped to his knees, and splashed cold water onto his face, then drank. Standing, placing his hat low over his eyes, he made his way to town.

He felt tired and had a headache, but otherwise his mind was fairly clear. He remembered the drinking he'd done the previous night and cursed himself for being a drunken fool.

A cat on a fence watched him approach. He dusted off his shirt and jeans, and readjusted the black bandanna around his neck. His stomach growled and he needed something to eat.

He walked down the main street of town, and a few stores were open. Ladies carried market baskets along the sidewalks, and drunks slept on a few of the benches. Stone saw a small figure seated on the edge of the sidewalk in front of the stagecoach office.

It was Lady Diane Farlington in her oversized cowboy outfit, her big hat on the back of her head, gnawing a loaf of bread.

"Howdy," she said. "Looks like we're the first ones here."

"Where'd you get that bread?"

She tore off half of it. "Here."

He accepted it and took a famished bite. She tossed him a wedge of cheese.

"Help yourself, pardner," she said.

He pulled a knife out of his boot and cut a wedge off the cheese. Standing before her, he ate breakfast. At her feet was a leather knapsack and a canteen. She drank some water and tossed him the canteen. It was full of hot coffee.

"I saw a solicitor last night," she said. "Thought his wife'd murder me, but he agreed to take the case. He told me basically what you said—that the district judge would come to town in a few days and let Paul go. There's nothing more I can do, so I thought I'd ride with you to Santa Fe and get your story, if you don't mind."

"I don't feel much like talking."

"I'll get you in the mood, don't worry about that. What's that over there?"

Stone turned toward the Carrington Hotel and saw a procession approaching. Edward McManus the banker was in front, smoking a fat black cigar, followed by Maureen and three hotel employees carrying two large suitcases each.

Stone's eyes widened when he saw his lost saddlebags hanging over McManus's arm.

"You left this underneath our table last night," McManus said. "Held on to them for you."

Stone thanked him as he accepted his saddlebags. He'd thought they'd be in Guadalajara by now, but they were safe, with his dirty clothes, his razor, and his canteen.

Mrs. McManus approached, a faint smile on her face. "I found them," she said. "You should thank me, not him."

"Thank you."

She winked, and he turned away, heading toward the nearest saloon. "Don't let the stage leave without me," he said over his shoulder. He entered the saloon, and the bartender was sweeping behind the bar.

"Could you fill this canteen with water," Stone said.

The bartender took the canteen and filled it from a pitcher. Stone rolled a cigarette and lit it. The bartender returned with the canteen. "Anything else."

"Whiskey."

The bartender poured the drink. Stone looked at it, hesitating. He knew he had to stop drinking. But just one drink wouldn't hurt, and it'd be a long journey.

He raised the drink to his lips, paused, then poured every drop down his throat. He stood stiff as a board for a few moments, then sucked wind between his clenched teeth and walked away, stuffing his canteen into his saddlebags.

He returned to the street. Banker McManus was looking at his watch. "Stagecoach is late," he said.

Stone walked into the stagecoach office. A man wearing a green visor on his head sat behind the counter.

"Why's the stagecoach late?" Stone asked.

"It's the Pitkin Overland Line and they're always late. They're gonna go outta business any minute."

Stone paid his fare and walked outside, sitting on a bench, smoking his cigarette. Diane lifted her knapsack and approached him. "You look like you slept in the street."

"I did."

"There wasn't much holding you up when you left last night. Do you always drink like that?"

He puffed his cigarette and looked up the street. Walking down the planked sidewalk, carrying a carpetbag, was the blond woman whom Stone had seen in the room across from his in the boardinghouse last night.

"Is this where the stagecoach is leaving from?" she asked.

"Yes."

She bent forward and peered at Stone. "I know you. You're the cowboy who made the big ruckus last night."

"Morning," said Stone, tipping his old Confederate cavalry hat.

"Where did you spend the night?"

"In the street," answered Lady Diane.

"No," said Stone, "on the sage, actually."

"You look rather filthy."

"I don't believe we've met," Diane said.

"I'm Priscilla Bellevue."

A rickety stagecoach pulled by eight old horses turned the corner and creaked toward them. Sitting atop the box, the reins in his hand, was a spidery old man with a long white beard, wearing a black hat with a chunk torn out of its brim.

Stone watched as the stagecoach came closer. It rocked from side to side and paint peeled from its sides. One wagon wheel seemed more oblong than round. A squeaking grinding sound came from one of the other wheels. Painted in faded gold letters on the door was:

PITKIN OVERLAND

"It's not going to make it," Stone muttered.

The old man pulled back on the reins and stopped the stagecoach. He yanked back the long brake lever, tied the reins to it, and climbed atop the baggage section.

"Got bad news for you folks," the stagecoach driver said. "This stagecoach cain't leave without a shotgun guard, and he's sick."

"Hire somebody else!" shouted Edward McManus.

"I cain't guarantee nothin'," said the stagecoach driver.

Stone wanted to be on his way. "How about me?"

The stagecoach driver looked at him. "Eight dollars a week."

"I'll take it."

The stage driver cupped his hands around his mouth. "All aboard for Santa Fe!"

The passengers climbed aboard. Stone made his way to the roof, the saddlebags over his shoulder. He sat on the box beside the stagecoach driver.

"I'm John Stone."

"Ray Slipchuck. Here's yer shotgun. If we have any trouble,

I'll 'spect you to stand and fight. If you run away, I'll plug you dead game."

A big cowboy hat and brunette tresses appeared above the roof of the cab. "I say there—do you mind if I join you?"

Slipchuck turned around. "Who the hell are you?"

"Just call me Diane. I'd like to ride up here. Is there an extra charge?"

"No ladies permitted up here, if you don't mind, missy—you are a missy, ain't you?"

"There seems to be ample room."

"You'll fall off."

"If you don't fall off, I won't fall off."

Slipchuck made the ugliest face he knew. "Young lady, I'm orderin' you to go below."

"There's no law that says I can't ride up here. I've already offered to pay any extra charges I might incur. If you want me to go down there, you'll have to carry me down bodily."

Slipchuck frowned as Diane made herself comfortable against the bags and boxes.

"Lovely view from up here," she said. *"Five Hundred Miles from the Top of a Stagecoach.* I can see the headline now."

Slipchuck looked at his pocket watch. "We'll wait another little while," he said.

In the cab, Edward McManus opened a picnic basket and took out a Mexican blood sausage, holding it in his fist and biting off an end. Maureen McManus, badly hung over, reached for the jug of hot coffee. Priscilla Bellevue stretched out her long legs and placed her feet on the empty seat opposite her.

"Care for some food?" McManus said to her. "We've got plenty."

"I've already had breakfast, thank you."

He leaned toward her, grease glistening on his lips. "Where are you headed?"

"Texas."

He winked. "Got a beau waiting for you there?"

"I've got a job waiting for me there. I'm a schoolteacher."

"Don't figure that pays much."

She smiled. "In my line of work, Mr. McManus, the financial recompense is secondary to the rewards of molding the minds of our children."

On the cab, Slipchuck looked at his watch. "Guess it's time to leave."

"You think those horses can make it all the way to Santa Fe?"

"They've made it before."

"Don't think I've ever seen such a broken-down rig."

"Pitkin Overland ain't doin' so good," Slipchuck said. "The problem is old Pitkin himself. He spends his money on his girlfriend instead of the stage line. They live on the whole top floor of the King Hotel in Denver—I seen him up there a few times, but listen—it's a job. It's hard for an old feller like me to find work these days."

Stone placed his hand on Slipchuck's shoulder. "We'll make it to Santa Fe together, Slipchuck. I'm proud to be here with you. Let's hit the trail."

Slipchuck pushed forward the brake lever and flicked the reins. The horses strained against their harnesses, and the stagecoach jangled and creaked as it moved forward.

"This is *so* exciting!" Lady Diane said, looking from side to side, sitting with her feet sprawled in front of her and her back against the luggage. "A stagecoach ride! Who could've imagined it!"

The stagecoach rolled out of town. Three small boys ran alongside the coach until it came to the open sage, then stopped and watched it move away toward the mountains, their hands shielding their eyes from the bright sun.

Stone rolled a cigarette and lit it, looking ahead at the wide plateaus and slow lift of uplands dotted with purple and gold. He realized he was feeling much better.

"God—what country!" Lady Diane said, spreading out her arms. "I've never seen anything like it. It goes on forever. One can't help thinking there has to be a God, when one rests one's eyes on such a land." She looked up at the sky. "Look at those birds over there. What kind are they?"

"Buzzards," replied Stone. "Probably just finished gnawing on the bones of some traveler who thought God was out here. This is Comanche country, and Comanches love white women. Kidnap them every chance they get."

"What do they do with them?"

"Turn them into slaves."

"*I Was a Comanche Slave*. Sounds like a great story. Do

you think you could introduce me to some Comanches?"

Stone stared at her. Slipchuck said, "Ma'am, if we run into Comanches we won't have time to introduce you because all of us'll be daid."

She shook her head in dismay. "I can't understand why there's all this fighting out here. Why don't all of you sit down and sort things out? You have a beautiful country and you should all share it peacefully."

"The Comanche don't want to work things out," Slipchuck explained. "They just want us to git."

"Deep down everybody's reasonable if you approach them on their happy side."

"Comanches don't have no happy side," Slipchuck said. "All they want to do is kill white folks, and what Mr. Stone here said about white women was right. Them buck braves shore do like white women."

"You can't scare me, Mr. Slipchuck. It's all exaggeration, like a newspaper story."

"Wild Indians're only half of it. There's outlaws all over the damn place out here, one gang competin' with the other, and they never hesitate to pull that trigger, the sons of bitches. They'll take everything you own, tie you to a tree, and have their way with you."

Diane felt uneasy. "Most stagecoaches get through without a scratch, isn't that right, Mr. Driver?"

"Name's Slipchuck, and no, most stages have one kind of problem or another during your average trip. We can prob'ly expect something, ma'am. That's why I ast you to stay below with the others."

"This is my post, Mr. Slipchuck. I'm not moving." She turned to Stone. "Have you ever fought Comanches?"

"Don't feel like talking."

"I believe you've forgotten our business, the twenty dollars?"

"I told you I wasn't interested."

"On the contrary, you signed a contract."

"I don't remember signing any contract."

"You were inebriated at the time, but I have it here in my knapsack—would you like to see it?"

"Yes."

She reached into her knapsack, took out a leather folder,

and removed a document from it, passing it to Stone.

He looked it over, and sure enough his name was on the bottom. He didn't remember signing it. *I've got to stop drinking.*

"Sue me," he said, passing the contract back.

"I will. You can be sure of it. And you'll spend the rest of your life in prison, rotting away, but that can be easily avoided. Just tell me your wonderful stories about Comanches and Apaches, and all the men you've killed, and everything will be all right. I'd also be interested in your Civil War experiences, strategic analyses of the great battles in which you participated, personal recollections, and anything else you might want to tell me." She took her notepad out of the knapsack. "You may begin now with the Comanches."

Stone turned to Slipchuck. "Would you mind stopping this stagecoach for a few moments."

Slipchuck pulled back on the reins, and the horses came to a stop.

Stone moved toward her, and she looked at him coolly.

"What do you think you're going to do?"

He picked her up like a sack of flour and carried her down the side of the stagecoach as she kicked and screamed. Slipchuck tossed her knapsack to the ground.

"I am not accustomed to being treated this way! I'll telegraph the British ambassador in Washington! You don't know who I am!"

Stone deposited her on the ground, opened the door to the carriage, and pushed her inside. His strong hand made her sit opposite Priscilla Bellevue.

He looked into Diane's eyes. "If you bother me again, I'll tie you to your seat."

"Well," she replied, straightening her billowing shirt, "you needn't get huffy about it."

A hand appeared, holding a bottle of whiskey. It belonged to Edward McManus. "Captain Stone—have a drink!"

Stone accepted the bottle, drank some, and passed it to Diane. Then he slammed the door, climbing to the top of the cab. Diane sipped from the bottle and held it out to Priscilla, who shook her head. Diane returned the bottle back to McManus.

"He was drunk at our table last night," McManus said. "Talking about the war. Evidently he's seen a lot of action."

"What did he say?"

"Something about Manassas. Up North we called it Bull Run. First big battle of the Civil War, and he was in the middle of it. Said forty percent of his troop didn't come back, and his closest friend was killed at Yellow Tavern"

Diane took out her notepad. "What else did he say?"

On top of the stagecoach, Stone returned to his seat next to Slipchuck.

"She's a wild un'," Slipchuck said. "Bet she felt good in yer arms when you was carryin' her down. I was married to a wild un' once. Half Cherokee and half Mexican she was. We fought all the time, but I loved her with all my heart. There was nobody like her. I tell you—she could melt the meat off a man's bones."

"Where is she now?" Stone asked.

"Daid."

"How'd she die?"

"I shot her."

Stone stared at him.

"Came home early from a run, caught her with another man. Went fur my gun 'fore I had time to think, and shot both of 'em. They say a slice from a cut loaf'll never be missed, but I was hotheaded then. You know what it's like when you're young. Full of piss and vinegar. Always lookin' for a fight."

Stone gazed at the stagecoach driver and tried to see him as a young man, and somehow the wild spirit still was there, behind the crinkles in his leathery skin and the tobacco-stained beard.

"Got married a few more times, but you know, Johnny, all women do is nag. There's always somethin' they want. They never leave a man alone. In my 'sperience, the prettier they are, the more they nag. Now you take that young filly you just carried off this wagon. Pretty as a picture, but a pain in the ass."

Stone gazed at the unlimited stretches of sage. Something moved far off in the hills to his right, and he swung in that direction.

"See somethin'?" asked Slipchuck.

Stone peered through the clear, still air, but couldn't find anything. Maybe it was a bird or an animal passing by, or maybe a Comanche scout. "You have much problems with Indians?"

"Sometimes. Got an arrow in me back once. But they didn't kill me. They'll never kill old Slipchuck. I'll piss on their graves."

Stone looked behind the cab, and Clarksdale had passed behind the horizon. They were in the wild country now. Stone looked around and saw numerous ways to ambush a stagecoach traveling without escort. A stagecoach would provide a big target for Indian arrows.

"Any recent Indian attacks?"

"Last one was about a month ago. Indians're leavin' this country, because there ain't as much buffalo as they used to be. Road agents are our main problem. You be on the lookout for 'em. They was a robbery other side of Coburn Springs a week ago. But old Pitkin don't give a damn. He's up there in his hotel room in Denver, ridin' his young girl."

They rode all morning across an endless vista of basins and plains, beneath a cloudless sky, and in the afternoon stopped beside a stream for lunch. Edward McManus carried his food basket to the banks of the stream and opened it up, pulling out an entire roast chicken. He tore off a leg and munched into it, as Stone stood on top of the coach and studied the land.

There were trees and large boulders in the vicinity where an attacking force could take cover. He only had Slipchuck and McManus to help him, and wasn't sure how much help McManus might be. The women would pass the ammunition. They could hold off maybe five or six attackers, but more than that would wipe them out in a series of coordinated charges.

It didn't look good, but maybe nothing would happen. Maybe they'd make it to Santa Fe in one piece. He climbed down from the wagon and joined the others for lunch.

They were seated in a circle next to the stream, and birds fluttered in the bushes nearby. The air was fresh and pure, and Diane filled her lungs with it.

"I can feel the energy of the sun deep in my bones," she said, her eyes closed. "What a country this is. It's the last paradise left on earth."

"Watch out fer the snakes," Slipchuck said. "They're all around here. You git bit by a snake out here and you'll be in paradise all right. And don't wander too far away on yer own, because there's wildcats and bears that sometimes git persnickety."

Edward McManus uncorked a bottle of whiskey, and Stone watched as the bottle made the rounds of the group, passed from one person to another, and he told himself he shouldn't partake, because he'd been drinking too much lately, but when Diane handed it to him, he wiped the mouth with his sleeve and raised it to his lips, took two good swallows, and handed the bottle to Slipchuck.

With a demented cackle, Slipchuck raised the bottle to his eager lips. Stone scanned the terrain around him. He'd been shot in the leg by an arrow at a water hole once and ever since had been nervous around water.

Diane turned to Stone. "Have you changed your mind about our interview?"

"No."

"I think you're being mean."

Stone got up and walked away, carrying his bread and cheese. She scowled as he disappeared into the bushes.

"Forget about him," said McManus. "His kind never gives an inch. But there might be an even better story right here underneath your nose, and you don't even see it."

"What story is that?"

McManus pointed his thumb toward his vest. "Men like me are the real story of the frontier. The cowboys and cavalry soldiers are just pawns in the game. Great fortunes are being made, in timber, mining, cattle, and land speculation, and a wilderness is being tamed. Ten years ago, when I first came out here, I had only the shirt on my back and a letter of introduction from a friend. Today I'm a substantial businessman with vast holdings and interests. That's your story."

Slipchuck snorted. "Don't write about them bankers," he said to Diane. "All they do is steal from widows and orphans and my boss Pitkin. You wanna write about somethin', you write about the stagecoach drivers. We're the ones who see everythin' an' everybody. You know what's goin' on out here? The frontier is gittin' filled up with settlers. Pretty soon you won't be able to move without bumpin' into another critter. I agree with the injuns. Keep it the way it was."

McManus smiled and placed his hand on Slipchuck's shoulder. "It's too late," he said. "You can't stop the flood once it's begun. All you can do is profit from it. You should let me invest your money. I'll make you rich." McManus handed him a business card. "You send your money to me. I'll make it grow. You might become as wealthy as I am, Slipchuck. Wouldn't have to push stagecoaches all over creation anymore."

"I like drivin' stagecoach, Mr. McManus, but it wouldn't hurt to have a little money fer a change."

Diane wrote in her notebook. "What would you do if you had a lot of money, Slipchuck?"

"I'd buy me a young wife."

Her eyes widened. "You can *buy* a wife out here?"

"I know an injun with a daughter, and I could get him down to ten horses." A peculiar light came into Slipchuck's eye, and Diane turned away.

After lunch they hit the trail again, and soon came to a beautiful valley soaking in the light of the bright afternoon sun. It had no purple sage; instead there were scattered trees of white aspen and dark green oak.

Stone felt the sweat pouring off his body. He looked ahead at the horses, dragging their hooves over the dusty road. A huge cloud of dust billowed behind the stagecoach. They were all alone in the middle of nowhere, a tiny moving dot on the landscape.

Stone touched his breast pocket, where his photograph of Marie was ensconced. He felt impatient, the stagecoach was moving too slowly. He was anxious to reach San Antone, so he could see her again, if it was she whom the rancher in Arizona had seen.

He hoped and prayed it was her. If it wasn't, he didn't know what he'd do. Probably hit the trail again and keep looking. What else was there?

His mouth was dry, and he needed a drink. He pulled his canteen out of the boot and took a sip. He had a mild headache from the bright sun and the whiskey. He was drinking too much, and it bothered him to know he was unable to stop.

He kept saying he was going to stop, but when the whiskey came under his nose, he drank it. He always found a rationale.

They watched the sun roll across the sky and sink down toward the orange and red horizon. In the coach, Edward McManus and his wife were taking a nap, sprawled all over each other, mouths agape.

Beside them, Diane was interviewing Priscilla Bellevue.

"Why is it," Diane said, "that a pretty woman like you isn't married?"

"I could ask you the same question," Priscilla replied. "Why aren't you married?"

"Never found a man I loved enough. How about you?"

"There isn't much to choose from out here."

"I thought men greatly outnumbered women, and it was easy for women to get married."

"It is, if don't mind marrying a cowboy."

"What's wrong with cowboys?"

"Don't ever trust one."

"They're awfully attractive—some of them."

"They spend most of their time with cows and horses, and it effects their minds," Priscilla replied. "It's not uncommon for them to ride their horses directly into saloons, and fire their guns at the ceiling."

"I'd love to see something like that."

"If you're around long enough, I'm sure you will. You'll probably see one of them shoot another one, because that's one of their favorite activities too. Their other favorite activity is to get drunk and pass out. Their third favorite activity is lying to women. They'll say anything to get what they want. If you find one who goes to church, it's only because that's where a town's nicest young ladies can be found."

"I take it you're talking from personal experience?"

"Take it any way you like."

Diane looked out the window. "This country is a wonderland. A sunset like this can't be found anywhere else in the world."

"If you want to find out what this country is really like, you should get a job and live in a community."

"I have a job," Diane replied. "I'm a reporter for the *Morning Sentinel*. Tell me more about the cowboy you met in church."

"If he loved me, he would've married me. Don't ever trust a cowboy."

"Every one of them can't be bad."

"I never met a good one in my life," Priscilla said.

They heard the voice of the Slipchuck calling out to them from above: "Deadman's Flats straight ahead!"

Diane poked her head out the window into the darkness of evening, squinted, and finally spotted a tiny dot of light in the distance.

"Doesn't look like much," she said.

"Stagecoach stops usually aren't," Priscilla replied.

Seated atop the cab, Stone saw a huddle of small ramshackle log buildings emerge out of the night, and lights glowed warmly in the windows. Slipchuck drove the horses to the front door and pulled back the reins.

The stagecoach stopped. "Throw down the luggage," he said to Stone. "I'll take the horses to the stable."

Stone climbed back and heaved the luggage to the ground, then jumped down. Slipchuck drove the team toward the stable and Stone tossed his saddlebags over his shoulder, walking into the main building of the stagecoach stop.

It was a small room with tables and chairs. The walls were bare logs chinked with mud, and lanterns hung from the ceiling. The big black stove was to the right. Three cowboys sat at the table in the corner, getting drunk.

A man and woman worked at the stove. Stone hung his hat on a peg and sat at a table, taking out his bag of tobacco. The man brought him a bottle of whiskey and four glasses.

"Tom Backus is my name," the man said. "What's your'n?"

"John Stone."

"Related to the Stones down in Coyote Hollar?"

"Don't believe so."

Stone wetted the seam of his cigarette and lit it, then stared at the bottle of whiskey.

He knew he shouldn't touch it. He should give it up for a few days. It was making him sick and slowing his reflexes. He'd read it was bad for the liver.

With a sigh he reached for the bottle, uncorking it and filling a glass half full. There was a noise at the door. Maureen McManus entered first, followed by her husband.

"Already into the whiskey, I see," he said with a smile, pulling up a chair next to him.

Stone drank half the glass down, and it hit him like a bolt of lightning. He nearly fell off the chair. "What the hell is this stuff?" he said to Backus.

"Locally made," Backus said.

Diane plopped herself down on the other side of Stone and

reached for a glass. "Where's the food?"

Stone sipped his glass of whiskey. Backus moved tables together so all the passengers could sit together.

"What's for dinner?" asked McManus, looking toward the stove.

"Steak'n beans," Backus said.

Backus shuffled toward the stove. A mangy dog approached the table with suspicious eyes and looked up at Stone, who carefully patted his head, and the cur lay his ears back.

Backus brought the food. The beans were in a huge brown crock, giving off a cinnamon fragrance. The steaks were stacked on a platter. Mrs. Backus gave everyone a plate.

Stone picked up Diane's plate, heaped some beans onto it, and threw a steak over the top. Then he placed it in front of her. "Dig in."

She stared at the steak. It overflowed the plate and sagged onto the rough-hewn wooden table. She'd never seen such a steak; it looked somehow obscene.

"You don't have to eat it all," said Stone.

"How can someone eat any of it?"

He sliced into his steak. Slipchuck opened the door. "Save some fer me!" he shouted.

He sat at the table next to Priscilla and poured himself a glass of whiskey. "Here's to Pitkin!"

He tossed the whiskey down his throat, and his eyes steamed over. "Hot damn!" he said. "This is fine likker!"

Stone was on his third glass, drinking it with his meal as if it were water. He sliced off a chunk of meat and stuck it into his mouth.

Diane looked at him out of the corner of her eyes. The candlelight behind his head showed a noble profile. He was a war veteran, a lost cavalier. What would it be like to be loved by such a man?

He reached for the bottle and filled his glass. Next to him, McManus stuffed a massive piece of steak into his mouth and gobbled it down. Slipchuck swallowed baked beans, gravy spilling into his beard, which seemed a repository of all the meals he'd eaten lately.

There was no delightful dinner conversation. No one spoke about the hunt he was on last Saturday or the latest ball. These people were eating.

Lady Diane daintily cut off a slice of meat and put it in her mouth, chewing nonchalantly. *I think I've been holding myself a little too aloof*, she said to herself, and plunged enthusiastically into the food.

They ate noisily and drank heavily. In the corner the cowboys played cards, one of them hooting occasionally. Backus carried more bottles to the tables, while his wife washed the pots and pans in a tub on a stand.

The door flew open, and a big cowboy with a black beard walked into the room. He slammed the door behind him and staggered to the nearest table. "I just been fired, goddammit, and I been drinkin', and I'm gonna drink some more, ain't that right?"

Backus brought him a bottle. The travelers finished their meal, and Backus cleared the dirty dishes away, but left the bottles of whiskey. Everyone continued to drink. McManus went out to the privy. Diane, not accustomed to a steak the size of a small dog, was growing sleepy. *I wonder where the beds are?*

Somebody stared intently at her: the drunken cowboy who'd just entered the stagecoach cabin. "Howdy, ma'am—name's Holtzman."

Diane felt warm, and unfastened the second button of her shirt. Holtzman arose and walked toward her.

Stone saw Holtzman coming and didn't like the expression on his face. He lowered his hand toward his Colt. Then he saw Holtzman swerve to the side and move toward Diane.

Holtzman pulled up a chair and sat next to Diane. She turned and looked at him. His beard was matted, his eyes were bloodshot, and he looked as if he were insane.

She turned to Stone, and he was drinking whiskey, seemingly unmindful of her. McManus had returned and was pawing his wife. Priscilla had gone to the privy.

The cowboy stared at her, a bent cigarette in his fingers. "Miss," he said hoarsely, "kin I buy you a drink."

She turned to him and tried to smile. "No thank you. I've got my own."

"Let's go out back together, you and me," he uttered.

She gave him a look that indicated she held him on a level with rodents and other pests. Then she turned to Stone.

"Can you do something about this man?"

"What's wrong with him?" Stone slurred.

"He's bothering me."

Stone bent forward and looked at Holtzman who looked back at him, a string of spittle hanging from his thick lower lip.

"Who the hell are you?" asked Holtzman, wiping off the spittle and throwing it at the stove.

"I'm with her," Stone replied.

"How much you want for her?" Holtzman asked.

"She's not for sale."

Holtzman thought about that, still staring at Diane.

"Can't you make him leave?" Diane said.

"How?"

"Tell him to go."

"There'll be a fight."

"If you're afraid, I'm not." She turned to Holtzman and eyed him coldly. "Please leave at once!" she commanded.

He stared at the opening in her shirt. Her throat was smooth and white, and a sweet fragrance arose from her body. He felt she needed him, and he leaned toward her, placing his arm around her shoulders, puckering his lips. "I'm all your'n."

His breath was like a buzzard's, and his fingers were caked with cowshit. She screamed and jumped to her feet. Holtzman lost his footing and fell to the floor. Stone burst out laughing, spilling whiskey onto his shirt.

Holtzman heard the laughter, and growled. He got to his feet, staggered to the side, and looked at Stone. "What's so funny?"

"Let me buy you a drink," Stone said, knowing he shouldn't't've laughed.

"I asked what's so funny, you squirrel-headed sheep-fucker."

McManus stepped between them. "Gentlemen, I'm sure we can settle this amicably between us."

Holtzman pushed McManus to the side, and McManus went stumbling into a flour sack. Holtzman and Stone glowered at each other. Everything became still. The cowboys in the corner turned around in their chairs.

Holtzman, in his pickled brain, thought Stone was standing between him and the woman he loved.

"Git out of my way," Holtzman said.

"Sit down and have a drink," Stone said. "You're getting to be a pain in the ass."

Holtzman lunged forward and threw a long looping punch at Stone's head, and Stone ducked out of the way, but his timing was off and the fist smashed into his mouth. His head felt as if it had shattered, and he reeled backward across the room, crashing into a table and falling to the floor.

Holtzman advanced to kick Stone's head in, but Stone rolled over quickly and got to his feet. He saw Holtzman coming at him, threw a punch, and this time it was Holtzman who couldn't get out of the way. The punch landed squarely on Holtzman's nose, and cartilage cracked beneath Stone's knuckles.

Holtzman went flying backward and smashed into the wall. His knees buckled but he didn't fall. Raising himself to his full height, he reached for his gun.

Backus cracked Holtzman over the head with the barrel of his shotgun, and Holtzman collapsed onto the floor.

"Will a few of you fellers gimme a hand with him?" Backus asked.

Stone and the cowboys from the corner carried Holtzman out of the stagecoach stop, seating him on his horse. Backus kept his shotgun trained on Holtzman as he regained consciousness.

"You'd better ride on out of here," Backus said, "and if I ever see you again, you son of a bitch, I'll shoot you on sight."

Backus aimed his shotgun in the air and pulled the triggers. Both barrels exploded, and Holtzman's horse became alarmed. He galloped into the night, taking Holtzman with him, drunk and dazed, trying to hold on for dear life.

They returned to the cabin. It was time to go to bed. Mrs. Backus showed them to their room.

It was ten feet square, and had straw mattresses covered with burlap on the floor.

Diane stared at the room in the wan light of one lantern. "We're all going to sleep in here together?"

"That's right," said Slipchuck with a drunken grin. "Ain't that great?"

Diane didn't know what to do. Perhaps they'd let her sleep outside in the stagecoach, but there was the danger of Indians.

The same would be true of the barn. "I'll take this one," she said, sitting on a straw mattress next to the one Stone was reclining upon.

A peal of thunder shattered the sultry night air, and another followed, a rumbling that shook the ground beneath them.

"Sounds like it's gonna rain," said Backus.

Stone let out a snore. He hadn't even removed his boots. Diane picked up her blanket and surreptitiously smelled it. It had the aroma of an old shirt with a touch of pig urine blended in. She decided to sleep without it, and spread out on the mattress.

It had its own special aroma, something between an old sock and a haystack. She used her knapsack as a pillow, but soon felt cold. The temperature outside was dropping, and a few pats of rain fell on the roof.

Stone continued to snore. She heard the others sighing, wheezing, and farting, trying to get comfortable. Priscilla Bellevue said a prayer on her knees before going to bed, then crawled beneath her blanket.

Diane stared at the ceiling. *Here's your story, darling. The Wild West with all its authentic smells.* The Carrington Hotel in Clarksdale had been comfortable, but this was far beneath the standards she'd set for herself. With a rueful grimace, she closed her eyes.

A drop of water fell on her face, and she sat bolt upright. Another drop of water fell on her head. She looked up and realized the roof was leaking. With a groan, she covered her head with the filthy blanket.

It was pitch-black in the room. McManus was snoring, and Diane felt wet and clammy. She'd never gone to bed in her life without taking a hot bath. Rain fell heavily on the roof and plopped onto her blanket. She moved closer to Stone.

He mumbled something and threw his arm around her. At first she wanted to throw it off, but it was heavy and she decided to leave it alone. He moved closer to her, and she felt his body. His warmth chased the chill away, and he smelled like a man.

She cuddled closer to him and closed her eyes, drifting into slumber and dreams of the English countryside in springtime.

4

THEY WERE ON the road by seven o'clock in the morning, and the sun gleamed on the horizon directly in front of them, casting long shadows over the sage. Farther on, beyond a gradual slope, rose a gigantic rock formation like the supreme monument of a lost civilization. The blue sky was adorned with streaks of silver, and a lone eagle circled high over their heads, a dot in the endless sky.

Stone wiped his mouth with the back of his hand. His tongue hung out and he felt like shit. His head throbbed with pain. *Why do I keep doing this to myself?* With shaking hands, he rolled himself a cigarette.

"You ain't lookin' so good this mornin', Johnny." Slipchuck flicked the reins. "You look like sumpin' that's been shot at, missed, and then shot at and hit."

"Think I had one too many last night."

"I'm feelin' poorly myself. But that was some fine likker and you got to take it when it comes yer way. It's my belief likker keeps a man fit. Some don't agree, but I ain't been convinced."

Stone lit his cigarette. He felt damn near dead. It was hard to breathe and he was weak. *I'm killing myself.*

The sun rose in the sky. In the cab, everybody lay with their eyes closed, taking a morning nap, the carriage rocking from side to side on its leather thoroughbrace suspension.

Diane felt languid and lazy, a faint smile on her pretty features. She was remembering how she'd spent the night cuddled against the standoffish John Stone, and how good it'd felt.

A few times, underneath the blankets, their cheeks had touched, and he'd pulled her closer. He'd been drunk, and didn't know what he was doing, but their bodies had been separated by only a few thin layers of cloth.

Edward McManus was sprawled next to her, dreaming about a network of stagecoach stops throughout the frontier, where the roofs didn't leak and there were decent sleeping facilities for human beings. He saw settlements growing up around the stagecoach stops, and then villages and towns. There'd be commerce, growth, railroads, factories. A new nation would arise and challenge the world. And he'd be one rich son of a bitch.

Across from him, Priscilla Bellevue was reading the Bible, John 8:7, about Mary Magdalene.

> So when they continued asking him, he lifted up himself,
> and said unto them, He that is without sin among you,
> let him first cast a stone at her.

Priscilla felt a special affinity for Mary Magdalene. Priscilla had to leave the town where she'd been teaching because of rumors about her and a cowboy named Zeke. Decent God-fearing people didn't want a tainted woman teaching their children. Now she was going to a new town where nobody knew her, and this time she'd stay away from cowboys.

She looked across the carriage at Diane, and knew the Englishwoman was falling in love with John Stone, who, in Priscilla's eyes, was either a cowboy or a gunfighter, probably both.

She was intrigued by Stone too. He was courteous and obviously a well-educated man, yet carried two big Colts, was built like a lumberjack, and drank like a horse. No man could drink like that and survive.

She wondered what was bothering him, and wanted him to tell her his problems, so she could help him. They could sit quietly someplace and talk about life. She wanted to save him.

In the corner, Maureen McManus reclined on her seat, a frown on her face. She'd married her husband because he was rich and she was poor, but kept comparing her husband to John Stone, and her husband didn't come off so well.

Her husband was twenty years older than she, with a big potbelly, flabby jowls, and thinning hair. Every night she went to bed with him and made the best of it.

She thought it'd be nice to go to bed with a young man, like John Stone. She'd known a man like Stone once. His name had been Charley Russell and he'd been a gold prospector who'd searched all his life for the mother lode, but never found it, except in her arms.

They'd had good times together, but his future hadn't looked so wonderful, and then she met McManus, who offered her the moon, and she took it. Now she was a rich banker's wife, with the best of everything, but every night she had to go to bed with the son of a bitch.

John Stone reminded her of Charley Russell. They both had the same swagger and careless laugh. Each was good-looking, in a rough and ready way. And both were heavy drinkers.

Charley Russell was his most amorous when drunk. He became a naughty little boy. Her husband burped beside her, as he dreamed of cities in the wilderness. Maureen turned away from him. She didn't ever want to go to bed with him again.

They came to a vast plain of gently rolling purple hills with a distant mountain range on the right. The plain seemed to go on forever, and the stagecoach path was a straight line directly through the middle of it, disappearing into the far horizon.

Stone puffed his cigarette, and little white spots danced in front of him. His stomach was queasy and he swore he'd never touch another drop.

He'd been drinking for most of his life, even when he'd been a teenager back in South Carolina. He'd drunk at West Point and he'd drunk during the war, but he'd never drunk like this. It was getting out of control. He had to take hold of himself.

Everything went back in Arizona. He'd been shot in a saloon, and his shoulder still hurt whenever it rained, like last night. An old Army friend had been mutilated by Apaches. A young cavalry officer whom he'd recently met had been disemboweled by Apaches. His Apache friend Lobo had been stabbed through the heart by another Apache. Stone began to drink seriously in Arizona.

But Arizona hadn't been a complete catastrophe. In the Sonoran desert he'd met the rancher who thought he'd seen Marie in Texas. Maybe in a month or two he'd find her, and things'd be the way they had in the old days, before the war. Maybe his quest would soon be over, and he could live a normal life again. And maybe not. The woman in Texas might not be Marie, or if she were, what about her husband, the elderly gentleman Stone had been told about by the rancher?

"I think there's somethin' out there," said Slipchuck, leaning forward and squinting.

Stone looked straight ahead and saw dancing dots of light. "What is it?"

"Somebody's comin'."

Stone raised the shotgun, cracked it open, and made sure it was loaded. "How many?"

"Cain't see yet."

Stone leaned forward and narrowed his eyes. He hoped they weren't Indians. It'd be a rough go, if they were Indians. All they could do was turn around and make a run for it, but those old nags pulling the stagecoach would be no match for Comanche war ponies. The braves would fill Stone full of arrows and he wouldn't have to worry about drinking anymore.

"Looks like a wagon," Slipchuck said.

Stone peered ahead and saw a black dot followed by a puff of dust at the end of the road. He realized now that he should've made the trip alone by horseback, but hadn't felt up to it. He'd nearly got killed by Apaches when traveling alone on horseback in Arizona. There was no easy way to cross the frontier. Indians even attacked trains.

The dot in the distance grew larger, and he saw that indeed it was a wagon. It looked as though one person was driving it, and he was alone.

"Looks like a female," Slipchuck said.

The wagon came closer, and Stone saw a woman with long dark blond hair seated in front, wearing a gray dress, a farmer's wife or daughter.

"Wonder what she's doing out here alone?" Stone asked.

"Prob'ly lives around here."

There was a load of hay in back of the wagon, which was drawn by two horses. Stone looked around cautiously at the gently sloping hills. He turned his gaze back to the woman.

He could see her white apron, and she wore her hair in pigtails. She raised her hand in greeting as she approached the stagecoach. Edward McManus poked his head out the window and took off his stovepipe hat. "Morning!"

She manipulated her reins, and her horses advanced across the road, blocking the path of the stagecoach. The stagecoach's lead horses whinnied and raised their front hooves, pawing the air. Stone stood and brought around his shotgun.

A shot rang out, and the shotgun flew out of Stone's hands, making them sting. He turned to the right and saw a man lying on a hill, a rifle in his hands.

The hay moved in back of the wagon, and three men stood up, masks over their faces, rifles in their hands.

"Hold 'em high and hold 'em steady," one of them said.

Stone raised his hands. Seven masked men on horseback galloped out of the hills and headed for them, guns in their hands.

"What's going on!" McManus demanded.

Diane looked out the window, and her hair stood on end. Masked men with guns in their hands were riding toward her. She unbuttoned her shirt pocket, pulling out her derringer.

Priscilla Bellevue reached out quickly and held her wrist. "If you fight them, they'll kill you and maybe the rest of us too. The only thing to do is give them what they want and hope they leave quickly without hurting anybody."

Diane hesitated.

"She's right," McManus said, placing his hand on her arm. "You'll get us all killed. Let me handle this."

Diane dropped the derringer into her shirt pocket and buttoned it.

A voice said: "Everybody git out of that cab, with yer hands held high, and if anybody wants to be a hero, he'll be a dead hero. Let's go—move!"

Diane opened the door and saw fourteen masked men on horseback, their hats low over their eyes. Their guns were pointed at her, and she stepped to the side so the others could get out of the cab.

It was hard to see what kind of men the outlaws were, because of the masks. They were all dressed like cowboys, and the man who'd talked had on a black hat and a black and white checked shirt.

"You up there!" he shouted to the top of the cab. "Git down here so's I kin see you, and I got lead aplenty if anybody wants some."

Slipchuck climbed down the side of the stagecoach, and Stone followed him. Stone looked at the wagon in front of the stagecoach, and the woman stood with a shotgun in her hands, aiming it directly at him.

Stone and the others lined up beside the stagecoach, holding their hands in the air. An outlaw climbed up the stagecoach to the baggage platform and threw down the bags. Other outlaws dismounted and approached the travelers. The outlaw on the stagecoach threw down the strongbox, and it slammed to the ground. Another outlaw aimed his gun at the lock on the strongbox. The gun fired, rattling everybody's ears, and the lock exploded. The outlaw bent over and opened the strongbox.

"Chock-full," he said.

He dumped the bags of coins into burlap sacks. Stone saw his old saddlebags fall to the ground.

"Search the passengers!" said the outlaw in the black and white checked shirt.

Two more outlaws dismounted and walked toward Edward McManus at the end of the line.

"Yer money or yer life," one of the gunman said.

"Take the money, but leave the life," McManus said genially, raising his hands higher.

They frisked him, dropped his wallet into a burlap bag. They took his watch, ring and the diamond stickpin in his tie.

"No matter what a man does," McManus said, "he has to provide for his future when he's old. Let me give you my card. Invest your money with my firm, and you won't have to rob stagecoaches for the rest of your life."

Maureen screamed as she saw her beautiful dresses thrown onto the ground. An outlaw opened her jewel box and raised a pearl necklace in the air.

"Looka here," he said.

"Hurry up," replied their leader.

An outlaw walked up to Stone. "Nice guns you got there."

"I need 'em."

"So do I."

He pulled the Colts out of Stone's holsters and dropped them in the bag. The other outlaw took Stone's wallet out of his back pocket and threw it in the bag.

Stone reluctantly threw his coins into the bag. The outlaw moved in front of Slipchuck.

"Ain't I robbed you before?" he asked.

"Hard to say," Slipchuck replied. "Cain't see yer face."

"You'd better thank God you cain't see my face, becuzz if you did—I'd kill you. Throw everything you got into the bag, and I'll take yer gun if you don't mind."

The outlaw moved in front of Diane, and a chill passed over her. She reached into her pocket and took out her wallet, tossing it into the bag.

"It's a girl!" the outlaw said. "Where's yer jools?"

"I don't have any jewels."

"She talks funny too!"

"Hurry up!" said their leader.

Stone stood with his hands in the air, watching the leader of the outlaws, who spoke with a southern accent. Another outlaw moved in front of Maureen McManus.

He grabbed her necklace and pulled it off, dropping it into the bag. She noticed a third outlaw staring at the cleavage of her breasts. He winked, then moved to Priscilla Bellevue.

She was ready and had everything in her hands, dropping the meager pile into the bag.

"You look like a schoolmarm," the outlaw said.

"That's what I am."

"I hate schoolmarms."

The outlaws slung the burlap bag over the rump of a horse. The rest of the loot already was stuffed into saddlebags. An outlaw detached the stagecoach horses.

"You're not going to leave us out here without horses!" McManus said.

" 'Fraid so," the outlaw leader replied.

"But we have no weapons. There are Indians . . ."

"Tough shit."

McManus's lips turned pale. "You can't leave us like this!"

"That's what you think."

"Yo!" shouted a voice among the outlaws.

They turned around and looked at a tall outlaw wearing a black shirt with a row of buttons on either side of his chest. He beckoned to the leader, who wheeled his horse around and rode back to converse with him. They spoke in low tones, and then the leader rode to where he'd been before. He aimed his gun at Stone. "You're comin' with us," he said.

Stone was astonished. "What for?"

The outlaw leader turned to the man next to him. "Let him use yer horse."

"What the hell'm I gonna ride?"

The leader pointed to another outlaw. "Ride with him."

Stone looked up at the outlaw with the checkered shirt. "Why do I have to come with you?"

The leader pointed his gun at Stone. "Do as I say."

Stone wasn't about to argue with a gun. He climbed onto the horse and looked back at the outlaw in the black shirt with the two rows of buttons. There was something familiar about the way he sat in his saddle.

"Let's git out of here," the outlaw leader said.

The outlaws wheeled their horses around and touched their spurs to their horses' flanks. The horses leapt forward and broke into a gallop, riding away from the stagecoach, leaving the hapless travelers stranded in the middle of Indian country.

The travelers watched Stone and the outlaws disappear into the sage. McManus took out his silk handkerchief and wiped the perspiration from his face. "Friends, we've been goddamned lucky," he uttered.

"What about John Stone?" Diane asked.

McManus shrugged. "Maybe he was one of them."

"I find that hard to believe," she said, but doubt ran through her now as she thought of his silence, his drinking, his coldness.

Priscilla said, "We've got to think of something to do." She turned toward Slipchuck. "What do you suggest?"

Slipchuck rolled himself a cigarette. " 'Bout the onliest thing we can do, I reckon, is go back to that stagecoach stop we was at this morning."

Maureen McManus widened her eyes. "That's a long way off."

"You got a better idea?"

Maureen imagined herself being skinned alive by Comanche raiders. She turned angrily to her husband. "This is your fault!"

McManus ignored her. "At least they left our food and water." He picked up his overturned picnic basket. "How far do you think that stagecoach stop is?" he asked Slipchuck.

"Fifteen miles."

Diane looked at the stagecoach sitting forlornly in the middle of the road without its horses. The wagon driven by the woman accomplice of the outlaws was there too. She'd ridden off on a horse with the outlaws, and Diane wondered who she was and what her life was like. *What a story she'd be.*

"We might as well git a move on," Slipchuck said. "Ain't no point hangin' around cryin' in our beer."

They gathered together the food, water, and some of the clothing, making crude knapsacks from shirts and pants. Slipchuck scanned the horizon and wished the sons of bitches had left him his rifle. It was hog-butchery being in Indian country without a rifle.

They hoisted the makeshift packs to their shoulders and began their long walk back to the stagecoach stop. Slipchuck went first, the women were next, and McManus brought up the rear. The sun beat down on them, and somewhere it was beating down on the Comanches. They trudged down the long road, looking fearfully at the hills. Slipchuck thought they'd reach the stagecoach stop sometime in the late afternoon, if the Comanches didn't get them first.

The outlaws' horses had slowed to a loping trot, and Stone rode in the middle of them, wondering what the outlaws wanted with him. He had no money, and no one would pay a penny to ransom him. It was a mystery, and he was still hung over. His mouth was dry and he felt a worm boring into the center of his brain. He glanced at the outlaw in the black shirt, and it was clear now that he was the real leader of the group. He rode in front of the others, and evidently the one in the checkered shirt had just been following his orders. Occasionally the outlaw in the black shirt looked back at Stone. No one said a word.

They came to a water hole surrounded by willow trees. Moss, lilies, and ferns overhung its green banks. The outlaws dismounted and led their horses to the water. Stone did the same, and noticed the outlaw in the black shirt walking toward him. Stone stiffened, moving his hands toward his empty holsters. The outlaw chief stopped in front and looked him in the eyes. Stone gazed back, and there was something about the outlaw chief's dark brown eyes that nagged his memory.

"Don't you recognize me, Johnny?" the outlaw chief asked.

The voice reminded Stone of the war. The outlaw chief hooked his forefinger into the black bandanna that covered his face and pulled the bandanna down.

"Now do you recognize me?"

Stone's jaw dropped open. "Beau!"

Beau held out his hand. "Good to see you again, Johnny. It's been a long time."

Stone stared at him. It was Captain Beauregard Talbott, who'd commanded Troop D in the Hampton Brigade during the war.

"Aren't you going to shake my hand?" Beau asked with his old roguish grin.

Stone shook his hand. "By God, I never thought the next time we met, you'd be robbing me."

"Imagine how I felt," said Talbott, "when I saw you climb down from the top of that stagecoach. How've the years been treating you, Johnny?"

"Just fine," said Stone, both men knowing it was a lie.

Beau looked at the outlaws gathered around them, and they too were pulling down their masks. "I'd like you all to meet the bravest man I ever knew—Captain John Stone, formerly of the Hampton Brigade. We're lucky we had the odds on him today."

The outlaws smiled faintly at Stone.

"These men were with me in the war," Beau explained. "Bobby Lee surrendered, but we never did."

The outlaw in the black and white checkered shirt stepped forward, his jowls covered with dark stubble.

"We best git movin', Beau."

Beau turned to Stone. "May I present my former first sergeant, Bradford Cavanaugh."

"It's a mistake—takin' him along," Cavanaugh scowled. "He ain't gonna be nothin' but trouble."

"It's all right, Cavanaugh. I'll vouch for him."

Cavanaugh muttered something incomprehensible as he walked back to his horse.

"He has a naturally suspicious nature." Beau smiled. "Life's a little strange when you're on the dodge. Care for some corn whiskey?

Beau flipped him his canteen, and Stone unscrewed the cap. "What do you plan to do with me?"

"We'll palaver for a few days, and then I'll set you loose."

Cavanaugh spoke from atop his saddle. "I don't think we should show him where the hideout is. He can bring the law down on us."

"Johnny, pass Cavanaugh the canteen when you're finished. I think he needs a drink."

Stone guzzled a few swallows of corn whiskey, then tossed the canteen to Cavanaugh.

"What've you been doing with yourself, Johnny?" Beau asked.

"Drifting and drinking."

"Times sure have changed, haven't they?"

Stone looked at Beau and remembered how splendid he'd looked in his officer's uniform, his cavalry saber at his side. Now Beau was unshaven, had lines of care on his face and weariness in his eyes.

"It's a new world," Stone said.

"New but not better." Beau looked around. "Where's Gloria?"

The outlaws made way for the woman who'd driven the decoy wagon.

"This is Gloria," Beau said, placing his arm around her shoulders. "She's as good a shot as any man in Troop D ever was. We'd like you to have dinner with us tonight."

"My pleasure," Stone said.

"Let's move out," Beau replied. "We've got a long way to go."

"May I have my guns back, Beau?"

"Sure, Johnny. Give him his guns back, boys."

"Now wait a minute," Cavanaugh said.

Beau turned to Cavanaugh, captain to sergeant: "Do as I say!"

A burlap bag was brought forward and dropped in front of Stone. He reached inside, searched among the coins and baubles, and found his two Colts. Spinning the cylinders, he dropped them into their holsters. The other outlaws mounted up. Beau and Gloria rode side by side to the head of the formation, and the outlaws moved their horses back to make way for them.

Beau stood in his saddle and looked around. He moved his arm forward, and the outlaw band rode away from the water hole. Stone closed his eyes, and it was the same sound as a cavalry unit moving to the front, the jangling and snorting of horses, the creak of saddles. *Time has turned me around.*

Stone sat tall in his saddle and looked ahead at Beau, leading the outlaw band just as he'd led old Troop D. Beau rode with superb form, his shoulders squared, a bandit by profession, an officer at his core.

Stone hadn't seen Beau since Five Forks in '65. The old First South Carolina had taken a beating that day, and Beau had been carried back to the medical tents with a bullet in his chest. Later, after Appomattox, Stone heard that Beau survived his wounds, but they'd never seen each other again.

Stone looked at Beau riding at a trot at the head of the outlaw band. Beau's hat was low over his eyes and tipped slightly to the right. Stone's mind flooded with memories that he usually was able to keep down.

At Chancellorsville they'd been surrounded by Union cavalry and had to cut their way out. At Antietam they'd been hit with an artillery bombardment that killed one man out of every four. In the Spotsylvania Wilderness they'd been overrun by Phil Sheridan's cavalry and nearly wiped out.

They'd been like brothers, and there were three of them. Ashley Tredegar was the third. He'd been shot out of his saddle at Yellow Tavern, leading Troop B in a desperate charge against entrenched Union infantry, and the whole damn thing had been for nothing, for a handful of sand.

Stone didn't like to think about Ashley, and in fact hardly ever let any memory of Ashley penetrate his mind. Ashley had been a fine human being, a real gentleman, and the bravest man in the world. It hurt too much to think of Ashley.

Beau loped along easily on his palomino, his golden tressed woman at his side. The outlaws followed him, John Stone with them, hoofbeats thundering on the ground, bringing the loot home.

They rode across a vast plain and disappeared into the endless rolling hills, a ghostly troop of old soldiers, who hadn't known how to surrender.

"I can't go on," said Diane. "I'm very sorry, but it's really no good."

She stopped in the middle of the trail. The heels of her feet were killing her.

Maureen wiped her forehead with the back of her hand. "I'm not doing so well myself."

"Neither am I," said her husband, soaked with perspiration.

Slipchuck frowned. "A fine bunch you are. Walk a few steps and you're ready to take a nap."

Diane sat down by the side of the road. "Just leave me here," she said wearily. "I'll get along somehow."

"So will I," replied Maureen, collapsing on the ground at the side of the road, her expensive low-cut green satin dress covered with dust.

Priscilla clasped her hands as if she were in a classroom. "We can't stay here," she said. "It's dangerous to be on the desert at night. There are wolves and wild dogs, not to mention snakes and scorpions."

"I guess they're going to get me," Diane said with resignation.

"And me," chimed in Maureen.

"My ass is dragging," McManus said. "Begging your pardon, ladies." He sat next to his wife, reached into his picnic basket, and took out a jug of water.

Slipchuck blew air out the corner of his mouth. He was getting annoyed with these people. They had no sand, no bottom, no nothing. The only thing to do was leave them here and go for help on his own.

He looked off across the sage, wondering what had become of John Stone. He'd liked Stone during the time they were together, though he hadn't been much of a shotgun guard. "You folks move off the road, into the hills there so's nobody can see you from the trail. I'll be back soon as I can."

Slipchuck turned and walked west on the road, a short slim figure with knobby joints, wearing a ruined cowboy hat. All he had with him was a canteen half full of water and a hide full of bad whiskey.

They watched him go. It was silent all around them, and civilization was far away. "Our lives are in the hands of that little man," said Diane.

McManus got up slowly, with many groans. "We ought to do as he says. Let's move away from the road."

"Help me up," said Maureen.

She raised her hand and he pulled her to her feet. Diane stood, and her heels felt as if burning coals were underneath them. Only Priscilla seemed unaffected by their tribulations, as God-fearing women sometimes are, to the annoyance of everyone else. But now she gave them confidence, as she walked erectly, carrying her Bible, the bun still neat on the back of her head.

They made their way into the hills and dropped down where they couldn't be seen from the road.

"All we can do now is wait," McManus said with a wheeze.

At this moment his investment portfolio seemed far off, but he reviewed his holdings anyway, like beads on a rosary. It was his only form of prayer, and maybe as good as any.

The outlaws rode across the sage, and Stone could hear the clanking and tinkling of stolen jewelry and coins. The men were in a good mood, talking with each other, laughing. They'd seen the money in the strongbox and were looking forward to a celebration at their camp.

They surrounded Stone, but he felt apart from them. He'd always managed to squeak just inside the law, and even had been a deputy sheriff once, but they'd chosen the other side of the law, and their leader was Beau Talbott from South Carolina, and that would take some thinking out.

Stone recalled the vast fields of cotton and his family's two-storied mansion with four white pillars in front. He, Beau, and Ashley had often sat on the back porch at night and looked at the stars, discussing the great things they wanted to accomplish when they were grown men, but they were hellions and drank anything they could get their hands on. Once they'd been jailed in Columbia for getting mixed up in a saloon brawl. In the Army, fighting had taken them over completely, and then there were no more plans.

Something died inside Stone when he heard Ashley had been shot. He'd found out about it during a lull in the fighting at

Yellow Tavern. Word had just been passed down that Jeb Stuart had been wounded seriously and was out of action. There was confusion about who was in command and what to do next, and meanwhile Billy Yank was massing for another attack.

A mounted courier arrived from Beau's troop with an urgent message for Stone. Stone unfolded the paper, thinking it was relevant tactical information, and instead saw only four words in Beau's handwriting: *Ashley has been killed.*

It was as if the sky had dropped on him. They were all soldiers, and knew they might die at any moment, but to have it really happen was something else. Now, even years later, Stone felt his eyes become hot. He'd buried these memories for years, but they had their own life.

He remembered how dizzy and sick he felt, and how his fighting spirit was demolished. He didn't want to go on.

Ashley hadn't been a normal human being. He had been more like a saint, always patient, always forgiving, never let you down. Ashley lived by his principles and would charge hell with a bucket of water. The Yankees shot him out of his saddle at Yellow Tavern.

Stone took out his bag of tobacco and rolled a cigarette, which was exactly what he'd done after he found out Ashley had been killed. Then the Yankee infantry launched their attack, and all he could do was mount up and lead old Troop C forward.

When he met Billy Yank on the plain, all he could think of was killing as many as possible, to atone for Ashley's death. He cut and ripped for a half hour, then had to fall back because there were too many Yankees.

There were always too many Yankees. That was the story of the war. But the war was over now for Stone. He looked ahead at Beau, riding proudly at the head of his outlaw band.

Evidently the war wasn't over for Beau.

McManus peered over the hill. "Something's out there."

Diane joined him and looked toward Santa Fe. She saw riders in the distance, headed in their direction.

One thing's certain, thought McManus, *they're not investors.*

"Think they're Comanches?" Diane asked fearfully.

"Hard to say at this distance."

She and McManus ducked down and joined Priscilla and Maureen sprawled in the shade of the hill.

"Keep low and be quiet," Priscilla cautioned them. "Comanches have sharp eyes and ears, and can smell white people a mile away."

Diane sat and looked toward the trail. She'd read about what Comanches did to white people. The blood drained out of her face.

"Are you all right?" Priscilla asked.

"I do believe I'm going to faint."

Diane lay down. It didn't seem like a great adventure anymore. *We should've stayed in safe cities on railroad lines,* she thought. *This was a mistake.*

It had been her idea to get off the main railroad lines and into the raw frontier. She'd been looking for the authentic American West. Now she'd found it.

Priscilla climbed to the top of the hill, looked toward Santa Fe, and saw two men on horseback. They were far away, and she couldn't tell whether they were Indians or white men. She prayed they weren't Indians, because Indians would kill them without hesitation, and they'd know white people were in the vicinity, because they'd left an easy trail to follow, and maybe that's what the Indians had done—followed them from the site of the stagecoach holdup.

The Englishwoman and Maureen could barely walk, and McManus was useless. They had no weapons, little water, less food. These might be their last moments on earth.

Priscilla had grown up on the frontier. Many of her friends, neighbors, and family members had died violently. She'd always known it could happen to her. All she could do was fight until she couldn't fight anymore.

She had no weapons except her hands, feet, and teeth. A person had to have faith in God. He would redeem her in the end.

She looked over the top of the hill again, keeping low as possible. She knew Comanches had sharp eyes, and could see anything that didn't belong on the sage.

McManus sat on the ground, his big belly hanging over his belt. The corners of his mouth were turned down and he thought he'd come to the end of the road. All his wealth and vast holdings didn't mean anything now. He felt sick, old, and vulnerable to attack.

They'd told him not to go on the trip, but he'd insisted that the frontier was generally safe for travel. He'd believed his own bullshit, always a mistake, he reflected now.

Maureen gazed at him with undisguised contempt. He looked defeated, tired, bedraggled. His stovepipe hat had a dent in it. *I hate him and I'm going to die with him.*

Priscilla observed the riders approaching on the trail. They were only a few hundred yards away now, and she thought she saw wide-brimmed cowboy hats on their heads.

Hope leapt in her breast, but then she remembered Indians sometimes stole cowboy hats from dead victims. She strained her eyes as she stared at the riders, trying to see what they were. She saw a plaid shirt, leather chaps, six-guns in holsters. A smile came over her face. They were cowboys! *God be praised! And please don't let them rape me!*

She took a deep breath and stood on top of the hill, waving her arms in the air.

Beau Talbott's band rode across a vast expanse of rock, bounded by a river that they forded. They passed through a wooded area, and then came to another river. Beau led them up the middle of it, against the current.

Stone knew they were making it extremely difficult to be tracked. He'd noticed the backtrailing, crosstrailing, and other maneuvers designed to lead pursuers astray. Beau was their commanding officer, with no real military rank. He held them together with the steel in his soul.

Stone heard a roaring in the distance. At first it was faint, like the wind, but then he realized it was rushing water.

The horses plodded up the river. Trees lined the banks, with mountains on both sides. Stone noticed the man called Cavanaugh glancing back at him, and it wasn't because he wanted to make a new friend.

They turned a bend in the river, and he saw a tall waterfall sending foam down the sides of a cliff. A rainbow arched above the waterfall, and Stone could see that this was where the river began.

Beau rode straight for the waterfall, and the outlaws followed him. A mist arose from the point where the falling water plunged into the river, and clusters of bubbles clung to the branches that lined the river.

"Just keep ridin'," said a voice next to him. "We're goin' right through."

The outlaws rode toward the waterfall, and pulled their hats tightly on their heads. Beau sat upright in his saddle, bouncing up and down, as if the waterfall weren't there. Beau's horse danced a few steps to the side, then walked directly into the waterfall.

Water cascaded down on Beau, and then he was gone. The outlaws followed him into the wall of water and disappeared. Stone could smell the cool moisture in the air, and the temperature dropped a few degrees as he drew closer. He took a deep breath and hunched his shoulders, and then the water pounded him; he couldn't see anything. It drenched his skin and ran down his legs, and his horse continued through the rippling sheets of water.

Suddenly he found himself in a dark passageway lined with jagged rock. Outlaws were in front of him, and light streamed in from the far end. The horses' hooves splashed in the water, and ahead of him Beau emerged into the sunlight.

Stone and the others followed him into a wide canyon with steep sides. He saw cattle grazing in the field, and cabins in the foothills, smoke arising from their chimneys. Stone stood in his stirrups and looked around. This was the outlaw hideout, and a damned good one.

The two cowboys rode closer, and were surprised to see what was in the hills just off the main trail.

McManus stepped toward them and removed his dented stovepipe hat. "Afternoon, boys," he said. "My name's McManus, and if you get us back to safety, there'll be ten dollars in gold for each of you."

"What the hell're you doin' out here?" asked Bob, one of the cowboys, covered with dust, a mystified expression on his face.

McManus explained the robbery and subsequent journey down the trail. "Can you go for help?" he asked.

"Why sure," said Bob. "Wouldn't want to leave you out here." He turned to Curly, the other cowboy. "One of us should stay here with 'em. You want to go for help, or should I?"

"Flip you for it."

Curly took out a coin, tossed it into the air, and caught it.

"Heads," said Bob.

Curly looked at the coin. "Tails. You go."

He showed Bob the coin, and Bob turned his horse around. "Be back as soon as I can!" he called as he galloped away.

Curly dismounted from his horse. "You had anything to eat lately?"

"Our food's gone," Priscilla said.

"Got some biscuits and jerky."

He opened his saddlebag and handed them the food. They sat on the ground and wolfed it down. McManus wiped his mouth with his handkerchief when he was finished. "That was mighty good," he said with a burp. "Glad you came along. We were worried about Comanches."

"That's nothin' to worry about." Curly rolled himself a cigarette.

"You're not worried?"

"I figure I'll see them 'fore they git too close, and I'll outrun 'em. Got me a helluva horse there. Might not look like much, but it's a helluva horse."

"Are you a cowboy?"

"Yes, sir. Work for the Double T. Lookin' fer strays, and found you instead."

"We're strays," McManus said. "Only we walk on two legs instead of four. How soon you think it'll be before your partner reaches civilization."

"Hour or two."

"I feel safer now that you're here with that gun."

Curly smiled. "This gun won't mean much if Comanches see us. Anyway, everybody dies sooner or later. Worryin' does no good at all."

Diane stared at him. He was an authentic cowboy riding the range, and her nose started twitching. "Where are you from?" she asked, reaching for her notebook.

They approached a complex of log cabins nestled in the lee of a mountain. Stone saw chicken coops, pens with pigs, and dogs running, barking, and biting each other.

Women and children came out of the buildings to greet the outlaws. Beau dismounted from his horse and then helped

Gloria down from hers. Help didn't seem to be anything she needed, but southern gallantry died hard. Stone climbed out of his saddle and touched his feet to the ground. Women and children gathered around the outlaws.

"Where's the loot?" one of the women asked.

An outlaw threw a burlap bag to the ground. "How do you like them onions!" Gold coins and jewels spilled out. The women and children rushed forward and plunged their fingers into it, shouting gleefully, like Indians with handfuls of beads.

Beau walked back to Stone. "Let's have a drink."

Stone walked beside Beau to the largest cabin in the vicinity. It was L-shaped, with a chimney in the middle. Stone couldn't help contrasting the cabin with the mansion where Beau had resided before the war. The Talbott slaves had lived in better places than this ramshackle cabin.

Beau opened the door, and they entered a rustic kitchen with a stove to the right and a round table to the left. Nailed to the far wall was a large Confederate flag.

"Have a seat," Beau said, hanging his hat on a peg. He took down a jug and two glasses from the cupboard, and set them on the table. "Help yourself."

Stone poured half a glass. So did Beau. They raised their glasses in the air.

"To Bobby Lee," Beau said.

Stone raised the glass to his lips. He knew he shouldn't drink it, but he hadn't seen Beau since Five Forks. It was corn whiskey again, with a kick like a mule. Stone's eyes crossed as it trickled down his throat.

"You could've knocked me over with a feather when I saw you on the stagecoach, Johnny," Beau said. "You don't look the way you used to."

"Neither do you."

"I was thinking about Ashley on the ride in. Too bad about old Ashley."

"Too bad about lots of things."

"You're a different man, Johnny."

"So are you."

"I'm still carrying on the fight, as you can see. It's only a guerrilla unit, but we don't take any shit from the Yankees." He raised his glass in the air again. "To all the straight-out

Southern loyalists who never caved in!"

They touched glasses.

"I've often thought of you, Johnny. Wondered what happened to you. You're welcome to join us. You can be my second in command. We could always use another good gun."

"I'm on the other side of the law, Beau. Not by much, but that's where I am."

Beau raised his eyebrows. "Is that the way you see us?"

"Men who rob stagecoaches are outlaws."

"We're livin' off the country, Johnny. That's the only way we can survive."

"The war's over."

"Not for me."

"I understand," Stone said, reaching for the jug.

"Do you really?"

"I think I do."

"If you understood, you'd join up with us."

"To rob stagecoaches?"

"I never surrendered," Beau replied, "and I never will." He sipped whiskey and stared at Stone for a few seconds. Then he said, "I'd like to show you something."

Beau stood and walked toward a doorway. Stone filled up his glass, guzzled it down quickly, and followed Beau into the next room. It had a few chairs and an old moth-eaten sofa, and then there was another door. Beau knocked on it.

"Who's there?" asked a woman's voice on the other side, and Stone's heart missed a beat.

"It's Beau, and there's an old friend of yours here."

She opened the door, and Stone found himself staring at Veronica Talbott, Beau's younger sister.

She looked at him with confusion, and he was shocked by her appearance. Only a year or two younger than he, she already had gray strands of hair, and there were dark pouches beneath her eyes. She wore an old party dress that was torn and patched, and a tarnished necklace around her throat.

"I don't believe I know the gentleman," she said in a plaintive voice, her brow furrowed as she scrutinized Stone. "Do we know each other, sir?"

"I'm John Stone," he said. "Don't you recognize me, Veronica?"

A muscle twitched in her jaw, and she looked to her brother for help.

"You don't remember John Stone?" Beau asked. "He was a friend of mine and Ashley's. You remember Ashley, don't you?"

"Of course I remember Ashley," she said with a smile. "You're always joking with me, Beau. Why, you know very well that Ashley and I are getting married in June. I was just writing the invitations when you knocked. The wedding will be a gala affair, I assure you. Even the Hamptons will be there."

"I used to bring you begonias from my mother's garden," Stone said to her. "I remember a pink dress that you used to wear, and you danced like a princess."

Her face became animated, and she took a step toward Stone, her fingers near her cheeks. "Johnny!" she said. "How kind of you to come! I was just having some refreshment—dandelion wine that I made myself. Would you care to join me?"

She led them into her tiny room. There was a bed, a dresser, and a chair. Stone and Beau sat on the bed. She poured them imaginary glasses of dandelion wine, and they pretended to take them from her hands. Then she sat on the chair and picked up her own imaginary glass.

"Ashley came to see me this afternoon," she said in a lost, vacant voice. "We went for a horseback ride down by the river, and then we had a picnic lunch, just the two of us. We're getting married in June, you know. I was just sending out the invitations. Everyone will be there, the very crème de la crème of South Carolinian society. We've hired a twenty-five-piece orchestra from Charleston, and the governor has indicated he plans to attend. We expect you'll be coming with Marie, Johnny. You know, Ashley was telling me just the other day how much he valued your friendship. He said there was no more gallant gentleman in the entire South. And by the way, why hasn't Marie come to visit? Has she been sick?"

Stone looked at Beau, and Beau winked at him.

"Yes, she's been sick," Stone said. "Caught a cold."

"Prettiest girl in the county, everybody says. Never a hair out of place. You're a lucky man, Johnny. There aren't many like her. I read in the paper the other day that the Yankees might actually invade South Carolina. What are your thoughts on that matter?"

"All I'm thinking is how lovely you look, Veronica."

"And you look glorious in your West Point uniform, Johnny. Some men are made for uniforms, and I guess you're one of them. I was talking with Ashley the other day, and he said he thought you'd be a general someday, but I told him no, you'll probably end up a planter like your father, isn't that so, Johnny?"

"I expect you're right, Veronica."

"Somebody was telling me something about your father, but I can't remember what it was. Something happened to him or . . . I don't know, sometimes I have dizzy spells. I don't suppose you ever have dizzy spells?"

"I have them frequently," said Stone, the corn liquor already hitting him.

"I haven't been feeling well, Johnny. Sometimes I have strange thoughts." Her face became serious. "I never remember them afterward, and I get headaches. Somebody was telling me something about your father . . . now what was it? Your father's all right, isn't he?"

"He's fine."

Her face became pale, and her hands trembled. She chewed her upper lip absentmindedly. There was a faraway look in her eyes.

Beau arose and took her hand. "Maybe you'd better lie down for a while, Veronica. You look a little fatigued."

She stared into space and didn't respond. He led her to the bed and helped her to lie down, covering her with a blanket. She closed her eyes, and tears rolled down her cheeks. Beau motioned toward the door, and Stone followed him.

"Sometimes she's lucid and sometimes she's not," Beau explained in the next room. "She was raped by a bunch of yellow-bellied Yankee soldiers and she saw Daddy get killed."

They sat at the table. A stout black woman, wearing a bandanna on her head, entered the room.

"Hattie," said Beau, "say hello to an old friend of mine, John Stone from South Carolina."

"Howdy," she said with a big smile. "Hope you're hungry, because we got a lot of food."

"I stay hungry," Stone replied.

Hattie lit the fire. Beau pushed the jug toward Stone and Stone refilled his glass all the way to the top, the sight of Veronica still in his mind.

Beau leaned toward him. "I can't forgive and forget, Johnny. I'm not made that way."

"I understand," Stone replied. He raised the glass and slugged the whiskey down. When he'd last seen Veronica, she was a vivacious girl wearing an engagement ring. Stone wiped his mouth with the back of his hand. "I can't forgive and forget either. But when Bobby Lee surrendered, that was good enough for me."

"He should never've done it."

"You used to call him the greatest military mind in history."

"He lost his nerve."

"I think he did what had to be done. The Yankees outgunned and outmanned us. It was futile to go on."

Beau shook his head sadly. "I never thought I'd see the day when Johnny Stone would bow his head to the Yankee invader."

"If Bobby Lee could do it, so can I."

"Bobby Lee was an old man. He'd lost his belly for war. What's your excuse?"

"I think he made the sensible strategic decision. The whole South would've been burned to the ground if we'd fought on."

"The coward dies a million times. The brave man dies once."

Stone looked up at him. "Tell me something—do you think Ashley would've joined you?"

"I know he would've."

"Somehow I can't see Ashley walking up to frightened ladies and saying: 'Your money or your life.' "

"Maybe you didn't know Ashley as well as you think."

"You and he were my best friends in the world."

There was silence for a few moments as both of them thought of Ashley.

The last night they'd been together had been the night before Ashley had been killed. They'd attended a meeting at Wade Hampton's headquarters, and afterward drank together from a flask in back of the picket line.

A full moon had been in the sky, and it cast a wan glow on Ashley's face. Ashley had been tall and lean, with wavy blond hair and a finely chiseled profile. They finished the flask and said good-bye to each other, shaking hands as cannons fired in the distant fields.

Then, out of nowhere, Ashley had given them the paraphrase of a quote from Shakespeare's *Julius Caesar*: "If we meet again, we shall smile," he said mysteriously, "and if not, this parting is well made."

Stone didn't think much about it at the time. Ashley was always quoting Shakespeare, Sir Walter Scott, Robert Burns, or some other literary luminary.

But the parting had indeed been well made, because they never saw Ashley again.

Stone and Beau drank more whiskey, while Hattie prepared a meal at the stove nearby.

"Where's Marie?" Beau asked.

"When I returned home after the war, she was gone. Have you heard anything about her?"

"She was gone when I got back too. A lot of people were gone. Sherman destroyed everything. There was nothing left."

"Somebody told me she went west with a Union officer, and that's what I'm doing out here. I'm looking for her."

Beau shook his head in disbelief. "Marie'd never go anywhere with a Union officer. She was the truest of the true daughters of the South."

"Met a man in Tucson who said he'd seen her in Texas, and that's where I was headed when I ran into you." Stone pulled the picture of Marie from his pocket and passed it to Beau. "This is all I've got to remember her by."

Beau looked at the picture. "She sure was the prettiest girl in the county. All the rest of us envied you, Johnny. But she only had eyes for you."

"If she only had eyes for me, why didn't she send me a message or leave me a note, or something?"

Beau turned slowly and faced his sister's bedroom. He looked in that direction for a few moments, then faced Stone again.

He didn't have to say anything. Stone knew what he meant. Maybe Veronica's fate also had befallen Marie. Maybe Marie was wandering around someplace in her old party clothes, babbling about orchestras and dandelion wine.

Beau filled up their glasses. "There is no justice," he said. "There is no mercy. People have to choose sides. You're wondering where Marie is? Well, where am I, and where are you? Where are all the other lost knights who were chewed up and spit out by the politicians?"

"I run into them wherever I go. The frontier is full of ex-soldiers who don't know what hit them."

Beau reached across the table and placed his hand on Stone's forearm. "I wish you'd ride with me, Johnny, like in the old days."

"Can't do it."

"I love you like a brother, and I don't want to argue with you, but how can you live in their world?"

"It's the only world there is."

"What about my world?"

"I'm not an outlaw."

"We're not outlaws. We're guerrilla cavalry."

"Tell that to Sheriff Pat Butler in Clarksdale."

"Now there's a tough old son of a bitch." Beau laughed. "I bet he'd like to know where we are right now. You won't tell him when you leave here, will you, Johnny?"

"I'd never betray you, Beau. You know me better than that."

A strange smile came over Beau's face. "Do I?"

"You ought to."

The door opened and a young man with black hair entered the kitchen. Stone stared at him, because he was the same young man he'd seen running away that night in Clarksdale, the one who'd stolen the wallet from Jesse Culpepper in the pisshouse.

The young man looked at Stone, and a flush came to his cheeks.

"You remember my brother Ewell," Beau said.

"I haven't seen Ewell since he was a little boy."

Beau turned to his brother. "Shake hands with John Stone, Ewell. You remember him, don't you?"

"Hello," Ewell said, a frightened expression on his face as he extended his hand.

Stone gripped Ewell's hand tightly to indicate everything was all right; he wouldn't mention anything about the petty thievery in Clarksdale. "I remember when you were a boy," Stone said. "You had a red wagon you used to pull on a string. Guess you're not a boy anymore."

"He's still a boy," Beau said. "Got a long way to go before he can call himself a man."

The three of them sat at the table, and the room was filling with cooking odors. Hattie banged a pot on the stove and cursed happily. Stone raised his glass and took another swig. He realized he was becoming drunk.

Beau rolled a cigarette. He seemed pensive, fingering the square of paper filled with long shreds of pungent tobacco. "You know, you can say what you want about the war, about all the bad things that happened, but there was something in it that was wonderful. Do you remember Manassas?"

"How can I forget Manassas?"

"Do you remember our first charge?"

"I remember it."

A smile came over Beau's face. "It was you, Ashley, and I, at the head of old Troop A, with Captain Willard leading the way, Jesus—I can feel it now as if I'm there." Beau's face came to life, and seemed to glow from within. "The excitement . . . the thrill . . . I felt like a god, as if nothing could touch me, and the cannonades were firing, and the bullets were whistling by, men fell off their horses, and horses were hit by cannonballs, blood flying through the air, the incredible booming sounds, the bugles, the flags flying in the wind . . ."

Beau's voice trailed off. He looked out the window at the sky, thinking about the struggle that took place on the grassy fields by Bull Run. Stone took another drink and had to admit to himself that the charge had been rather tumultuous. There was nothing in the world quite like a full-tilt cavalry charge.

Beau turned around and faced him. "We won that one, and it was the first major battle of the war. Do you remember how it felt to be victorious? And they'd outnumbered us—you know they outnumbered us."

"They always outnumbered us."

"But we had better leadership. Bobby Lee, Longstreet, Old Stonewall, Jeb Stuart. Has the world ever seen, before or since, anything like them? Even our second rank of officers was first-rate: men like Dorsey Pender, George Pickett, and good old Jubal Early. And our enlisted men fought with more spirit, because they were fighting for their way of life, while the Yankees were just in it for the money."

"The Yankees believed in something too, Beau. You might not agree with them, but they had their own ideals, and sooner or later men with ideals start killing each other. Funny thing about ideals."

"You've gotten cynical, Johnny."

"I've grown up."

"I guess you think I haven't grown up."

"That's right."

"I knew you'd think that. That's the way your mind works, because you've been defeated. That's the difference between you and me, Johnny. You've been defeated and I haven't. You're walking away with your tail between your legs, and I'm fighting on."

"I saw you fighting on today, Beau. You pointed your gun at a bunch of women."

"We didn't hurt them. It's guerrilla warfare. Live off the land. You took the same courses I did at the Point. You know what I'm talking about."

"All I know is Bobby Lee surrendered, and I want to get on with my life."

"How can you have a life under the Yankees?"

"I get along all right."

"I'm sure you do, by licking their boots."

Stone got to his feet. So did Beau. They faced each other, gazing into each other's eyes. Ewell went white and pushed his chair back.

Hattie placed a baked ham on the table between them. "Here's supper," she said. "Ya'll better wash yo' hands. Nobody eats in mah kitchen wif dirty hands." She turned to Beau. "What's wrong with you, boy? I told you to wash yo' hands!"

Beau smiled at Stone. "You see the way she talks to me? Sometimes I think she's in command here, and I'm her executive officer."

He led Stone out the back door, and they washed in a basin on a wooden crate.

Beau slapped Stone on the shoulder. "Sorry about what I said in there. The heat of argument, you know. No hard feelings?"

"Hell no," said Stone, and wondered when the next volley would come, and how strong it would be.

Beau returned to the house, and Stone finished washing. He dried his hands on the same towel Beau had used, and stepped deeper into the backyard, looking around. The outlaws had their own little isolated world in the middle of nowhere, and there was only one way to get in or out—through the water-fall. He wanted to leave as soon as etiquette would allow. This wasn't the Beau Talbott he used to know. Or was it?

The back door opened, and Gloria walked toward him, wearing a long brown skirt that came to the tops of her boots. She was tall and rawboned, and he guessed her age at thirty-five.

She dipped her hands into the water. "So you're John Stone," she said with a smile. "I wish I had a dollar for every night Beau kept me up talking about you and Ashley."

"Where are you from?"

"Virginia. I met Beau in a hospital in Richmond, after he was wounded. I was helping the doctors there."

"I thought you were going to shoot me today."

"If you made one wrong move, I would've."

They returned to the dining room, and Stone saw a man holding a violin, standing against the far wall. Ewell brought Veronica out of her room, and she carried a tattered old fan in her hand. "I'm so glad all of you could come to dinner with us tonight," she said, her face covered with garish cosmetics. "I've made some special dandelion wine for the occasion. Governor Hammond said he might stop by later. Ewell you may tell the band to begin."

The violinist raised his instrument to his chin and drew back the bow, and Stone heard a Mozart concerto. Beau sat between Gloria and Veronica and Ewell was on the other side of Veronica. Stone dropped down next to Ewell, and Gloria was to his left.

In the middle of the table was a huge ham, sending tiny trails of clove-flavored steam into the air. There also were platters piled high with sweet potatoes, bread, and string beans.

They all bowed their heads.

"Lord," said Beau, "We thank you for the blessings of this table, and we look to the day that the South will be free again. Amen."

Beau picked up his knife and fork.

"That little prayer didn't bother you none, did it, Johnny?"

"No."

"I thought it might, since I imagine you're one of those who wouldn't want the South to be free again."

"That's not true."

"Why don't you prove it?"

Gloria turned to Beau. "I don't think this is proper dinner conversation, if you don't mind."

Veronica perked up her ears, and her eyes brightened. "Ashley was here this afternoon," she said. "He brought me a bouquet of roses. We'll be wed in June, and everyone will be there. Have you tried my dandelion wine?"

She stared into space, and a silence fell over the table. Stone remembered sitting to dinner with this very family in their plantation dining room before the war. A crystal chandelier had been overhead, and white drapes covered the tall windows. They'd been served by uniformed servants, and they all wore their finest clothes.

Now they were in a broken-down cabin chinked with mud. Ewell was a petty thief, Veronica had lost her mind, and Beau was an embittered fanatic.

Stone reached for the whiskey and filled his glass. The dream was over, and the nightmare had begun.

It was dark when they rode into Clarksdale, led by cowboys from the Double T Ranch. They'd been on the trail since late afternoon, and now it was almost midnight.

The townspeople and cowboys watched them pass, for they were a sight to behold: Lady Diane in her rumpled cowboy outfit, Maureen in her torn satin dress, McManus with his broken stovepipe hat, and Priscilla sitting stiffly in her saddle, her Bible underneath her arm.

They stopped in front of the sheriff's office and climbed down from their mounts. Sheriff Butler came out to see them, chewing a thin cigar, a frown on his face.

He led them into his office and sat behind his desk. "Where'd this happen?"

Slipchuck answered: "'Bout fifteen miles east of Deadman's Flats."

"And you say they kidnapped somebody?"

"The stagecoach guard, name of John Stone."

"Never heard of him."

"Hired him the mornin' we left. Nice feller."

"Know anything about him?"

"No."

"Maybe he was in with 'em."

"Don't think so."

"Why not?"

"Wasn't that kind of man."

Sheriff Butler looked up at him. His silvery hair was thin on top, and he had a nose like a hawk. "How do you know?"

Diane stepped forward. "Now see here. What are you suggesting? A citizen of your country has been kidnapped by desperadoes, and why aren't you doing something about it?"

Sheriff Butler turned to her. "Who're you?"

"I'm a reporter for the London *Morning Sentinel*."

"The what?"

"I've interviewed Mr. Stone extensively, and I assure you that he had nothing to do with this holdup."

"You don't know that." Sheriff Butler turned to Slipchuck. "What did this Stone bird look like?"

At that moment the Earl of Dunwich entered the sheriff's office. "Diane!"

They rushed toward each other and embraced.

"I've been so worried about you," he said.

"When did you get out of jail?"

"This morning. My solicitor took care of it. Just had to pay some money, like England."

"The sheriff thinks John Stone had something to do with the holdup."

Paul let Diane go and walked toward Sheriff Butler. "That's preposterous. John Stone is a gentleman."

"That remains to be seen," Sheriff Butler replied.

Edward McManus stepped forward, his banged-in stovepipe hat on his head. "I'm herewith posting a five-hundred-dollar reward for information leading to the rescue of John Stone."

"Make it a thousand," Dunwich said.

Sheriff Butler puffed his cigar and looked up at them coolly. "Let me get this straight. You two're postin' one thousand dollars reward for John Stone."

"That is correct," Dunwich said.

"Dead or alive?"

"We prefer him alive."

"What if he's part of the outlaw gang?"

"That's utter rubbish."

"What if he is? Will the reward still be paid?"

"Whoever brings him back will be paid," Dunwich said.

Stone staggered toward the bunkhouse. The full moon shone down upon him and he could see the mountains in the distance like the high walls of a prison.

Above him blazed the heavens, and a night bird called out from atop a cottonwood tree. All he wanted to do was go to sleep.

He advanced toward the door of the bunkhouse and opened it up, heard men's voices, then suddenly it was silent.

He stepped into the bunkhouse. A group of outlaws was seated around a table, and in the middle was a jug. The outlaws looked at him, and there was resentment in their eyes.

"Where's an empty bunk?" he asked.

Nobody said anything. He saw Cavanaugh at the far end of the table, glowering at him.

"If nobody'll tell me where an empty bunk is," Stone slurred, "I'll just lay my ass anywhere."

"Try it an' see what happens to you," said Cavanaugh evenly.

Stone looked at them. "Changed my mind," he said. "I'd rather sleep outdoors than with a bunch of thieving bastards."

The outlaws at the table looked at one another. Some were bearded, some had crude tattoos on their arms. Cavanaugh got to his feet and hooked his thumbs in his belt. "Who're you callin' a bastard, you damned turncoat!"

Stone drunkenly pointed his finger at him. "You."

Cavanaugh stared at him for a few moments, working the muscles in his jaw. "Maybe you and me oughtta go outside."

"Let's do it," Stone replied.

Stone turned around and reeled toward the door. Pushing it open, he stumbled outside and unbuttoned his shirt. Cavanaugh followed with the others.

The moon shone down on them as the outlaws gathered around the two combatants. Stone threw his shirt on the ground and turned toward Cavanaugh.

Cavanaugh was bare-chested, balling up his fists, cocking his head slightly to the side as he measured Stone. Cavanaugh had a black mustache and was thick around the middle, covered with scraggly hair. He looked strong and mean.

Stone flexed his fingers. The cool night breeze blew over him. He thought Cavanaugh would be armor-plated around the head, but slow in the legs. *I've got to keep moving on him, and don't let him bear-hug me.*

"We don't like turncoats and traitors," Cavanaugh said, raising his fists. "You're going to git the beatin' of yer life, boy."

Stone advanced toward him, holding his fists at chin level, looking for openings in Cavanaugh's defense.

"Kick his ass, Cav," one of the outlaws said. "Show 'im who's boss."

Cavanaugh and Stone met in the center of the ring and Cavanaugh pawed at Stone with his right fist, while Stone bobbed from side to side, but his reflexes were off and he looked like an awkward fighter.

"Show 'im what we think of cowards," another outlaw said. "Punch his lights out."

Stone knew the word must've gotten around that he'd refused to join the band, and they didn't like it, but he didn't like them either.

Cavanaugh wasn't as drunk as Stone. He saw that he'd have an easy time of it. He pawed with his left fist, then snapped it out suddenly and hit Stone on the nose.

Stone was stunned, and his nose trickled blood. If he'd been sober, he would've been able to get out of the way, but he wasn't sober.

Cavanaugh dug a left hook to Stone's ribs, and Stone blew out air, then Cavanaugh cracked Stone on top of his head.

Stone backpedaled, trying to cover up, and Cavanaugh smashed him on the ear. Stone heard bells and went down.

"Stomp 'em, Cav," somebody said.

A boot whacked into Stone's head, and he scrambled to his feet. Cavanaugh rushed him, tackled him, and brought him down. Stone landed on his back, and Cavanaugh was on top of him. Cavanaugh raised his fist and punched Stone in the mouth.

Stone knew he was in deep trouble, and went berserk. He

exploded off the ground, knocked Cavanaugh away from him, and managed to rise unsteadily to his feet.

Cavanaugh attacked immediately, throwing a left jab at Stone's eye and connecting. Stone moved his upper body from side to side, looking for an angle, and thought he saw one, but before he could get off, Cavanaugh threw a long overhand right, and next thing Stone knew he was lying on his back again.

He looked up, and saw Beau in the crowd, along with Ewell and Gloria. Then he saw Cavanaugh standing in front of him, his fists down his sides, his legs spread apart.

"Git up, you yellow-belly bastard!"

Stone had been in many fights, and knew all the outcomes. The outcome of this would be his own humiliating, bloody, and painful defeat, unless he could pull something out of the hat.

He knew he didn't have his usual fighting skill. His reflexes and timing were way off. But he had one asset: his physical strength. It still was mostly there, despite the alcohol, if he could get it focused.

He had a puncher's chance. Find an opening, or make one, and hit Cavanaugh with everything he had.

"Are you gonna git up?" Cavanaugh asked, "or am I a-gonna kick you in your big, fat yellow-belly head again?"

Stone got to his feet slowly. His face felt bent out of shape, and the taste of blood was salty on his tongue. *God*, he thought, *if you let me win this fight, I'll never drink again.*

Cavanaugh came at him, his fist in the air bare-knuckle style. Stone hunched over and covered up, peering through his guard at Cavanaugh, praying that God would give him that one opening he needed.

Cavanaugh shot a jab at Stone's head, and Stone picked it off. Then Cavanaugh threw an uppercut, and Stone leaned back out of the way. Cavanaugh rushed in, threw a feint at Stone's head, and Stone raised his arms to block the punch that never came.

A different punch came instead. It was a solid hook to Stone's kidney, and Stone thought he'd pass out from the pain. But he held steady and took punishment as Cavanaugh hammered his body again and again. Cavanaugh stepped back and looked at Stone, and Stone was bent over, his guts and ribs hurting.

"There ain't much to you," Cavanaugh said. "Never is much—with traitors."

He moved in more confidently, aimed a jab at Stone's forehead, and connected. Stone saw stars, and then another fist rammed into his mouth, knocking his teeth loose, and his mouth filled with blood. He went reeling backward fell into a group of outlaws, and with a whoop they pushed him back at Cavanaugh, who was waiting, measuring, loading up.

Cavanaugh shot his fist forward like a rocket, and it struck Stone on the chin. Stone went flying backward and landed on his ass.

Cavanaugh undulated before him, and Stone heard somebody laugh. Blinking, trying to clear out the cobwebs, he saw Beau watching in the crowd. Stone tried to get up but his legs couldn't do it. He looked at Cavanaugh.

"Stomp him, Cav."

Cavanaugh stepped forward, and one of his black boots flew toward Stone's head. Stone lurched forward, tackled Cavanaugh, and brought him down. Both men spun away from each other and got to their feet but Cavanaugh was up first, and he kicked Stone in the chops.

Stone went flying backward again, landing on the ground. Cavanaugh charged and Stone knew he couldn't get out of the way.

Cavanaugh kicked, and Stone caught his boot in the air, twisting to the side. Cavanaugh lost his balance and fell, as Stone got up, swayed, and raised his fists. Cavanaugh climbed to his feet. They faced each other again, breathing heavily.

Stone didn't think he could carry on much longer. *It's now or never*, he thought.

Stone threw his massive bulk at Cavanaugh, and Cavanaugh stepped to the side. Stone stumbled over his feet, lost his balance, and fell to the dirt.

Everybody laughed. Stone pulled himself up and turned around. It was getting worse. He hurt all over. *Just give me one good punch.*

"Finish 'im off!" somebody said.

Cavanaugh stepped forward, and Stone knew this was it.

Somehow he had to hit Cavanaugh solidly, but Cavanaugh always landed the first punch, and if Cavanaugh hit him again, it'd be the end of the fight. Stone was groggy and the ground rocked beneath him like the deck of a ship in heavy seas. Cavanaugh inched closer, and was about to let fly, when Stone grit his teeth and cut loose.

Cavanaugh was in the middle of his swing when Stone's right fist came streaking out of the night at him, and Cavanaugh thought a mountain fell on his head. Everything went black, and Cavanaugh's knees buckled. Stone took a step back and blinked. Cavanaugh was motionless, his legs paralyzed, holding his hands feebly near his face.

Stone knew it was a good punch as soon as it landed. It had felt solid all the way down to his toes, with all his weight behind it. *Thank you, Lord*, he thought, and gleefully slammed Cavanaugh in the gut. Cavanaugh expelled air through all his orifices, and threw a wild looping right at Stone's head, which connected, but had no real steam on it.

Stone recovered quickly, knew he had his man hurt, and went in for the kill. He threw the most devastating punch in his arsenal, a swooping straight right with all his weight behind it, and it landed on Cavanaugh's nose.

Blood poured down Cavanaugh's throat, choking him as he tried to breathe. Stone slammed him again, and Cavanaugh fell back against the edge of the corral.

Stone hit him with a left and a right, and Cavanaugh dropped lower. Then Stone took aim and threw his favorite punch again, and it connected solidly with Cavanaugh's mouth.

Cavanaugh's legs gave out, and he collapsed onto the ground. He rolled onto his back and lay still, his face a mask of blood.

Stone stood over him, sucking wind. It was clear that Cavanaugh wouldn't get up for a long time. Then he turned around and faced the outlaws standing solemnly in the moonlight.

"I'd rather sleep with the buzzards!" Stone hollered at them.

Turning around, nearly stumbling over his own feet, he walked off into the sage. They watched the night close around him, and then he was gone.

5

JOHN STONE OPENED one eye. He saw a patch of grass and a creature standing beyond it. Opening his other eye, he raised his head a few inches off the ground.

A gopher stood in front of him, its paws in a prayerful position, looking at him curiously. Stone blinked his eyes. *Where am I?*

He pulled himself to a sitting position, spit something foul out of his mouth, and looked around.

He was in the sage wilderness, and mountains sprawled in the distance. He had no bedroll, no saddle for a pillow. His memory was a blank.

A dull ache came from his left cheek, and then he remembered everything in a rush: the fight, the reunion with Beau, the stagecoach holdup.

He groaned and got to his feet. His body felt as if a herd of crazed cattle had run over him. His chest hurt every time he took a breath. Waves of pain rolled across his brain.

He saw a trail of smoke rising in the air, and made his way toward it. Every step increased the pain and pressure in his head, and he was sure he had at least one fractured rib. His kidney felt as if somebody had stuck a knife into it and was twisting it around. He looked at his knuckles, and they were skinned. There were sharp pains in his right hand, where he'd hit Cavanaugh with everything he had.

He'd never taken such a beating in his life.

He walked around a tree and saw Veronica wearing one of her old party dresses, tenderly picking a wildflower. She raised it to her nose, and an expression of bliss came over the thick mask of cosmetics on her face.

"Good morning, Veronica," Stone said as he approached her, dried blood all over him.

She turned toward him and smiled. "Oh—good morning, Johnny. How was the hunt? Did you get anything?"

"No."

"Have you seen Ashley?"

"He—he went to buy a new horse."

"He hasn't come back yet. I wonder where he is. I haven't been feeling well lately, Johnny. The political situation has me awfully worried. Do you think there'll be war?"

"I don't know."

"Ashley says it's inevitable." An expression of consternation came over her face, but then she smiled. "I shouldn't worry so much, because we'll be able to beat the damned Yankees, won't we?"

"I hope so, Veronica."

Her smile faltered. She looked confused and frightened, her eyes darting around Stone's battered face. Then a smile slowly spread onto her grotesque face. "I hear Ashley," she whispered. "He's calling me." She cupped her hands around her mouth. "I'm coming, Ashley!" Then she looked at Stone. "Excuse me, Johnny, but Ashley wants me. You know what he's like—he can't seem to do anything without me."

She lifted her skirts and ran off into the sage, calling Ashley's name.

Stone shook his head as he continued toward the scattering of cabins. He saw a stout woman bending over a washtub in a backyard. A few men sat in front of the bunkhouse, smoking cigarettes. They looked up at him as he passed, and he ignored them.

He made his way to the back of Beau's cabin, and filled the pitcher with water from the well. Then he washed his face, and saw the clear water become dark and clouded. He was sure his nose was broken. His lip was cut badly. He heard bells ringing in his left ear.

He dried his face on the towel, put on his hat, and entered

the cabin. Beau and Gloria sat at the kitchen table, drinking coffee and reading old newspapers.

"They finally finished the transcontinental railroad," Beau said. "A golden spike, connecting the rails from east and west, was driven at Promontory Point, Utah, last May tenth. Now you can travel by train all the way across the country."

Stone sat at the table and looked at the jug of whiskey in the middle.

Gloria took a covered plate out of the oven and placed it in front of Stone. Then she poured him a cup of coffee. Stone took the cover off the plate and saw thick slices of bacon, scrambled eggs, grits, and biscuits. Suddenly he became aware of a cavern in his stomach. He reached for the silverware.

Beau lay the newspaper on the table and watched Stone eat. "You took a lot of punishment last night."

"I was too drunk to get out of the way."

"I thought he had you."

"So did I."

"You're the first man who's ever beaten Cavanaugh in a fight in all the years I've known him."

"They all think I'm a traitor, and that's what you think too, right?"

"You surrendered, and you shouldn't've."

"I didn't surrender last night."

Stone ate his breakfast and drank his coffee. Beau and Gloria returned to their newspapers.

Beau lit a cigar. "Just what we need—a transcontinental railroad. Pretty soon everybody will have a depot in his backyard. A man won't be able to take a step without bumping into somebody. Is that supposed to be progress?"

Stone finished his food and pushed the plate away. Gloria refilled his cup with coffee. Stone felt better; his strength was returning. He rolled a cigarette.

"When can I get out of here?" he asked.

"What's your hurry?"

"I don't want to get shot in the back by one of your noble Galahads out there."

"I've issued orders that they should leave you alone. You'll be all right from now on."

"I'd like to get moving."

"You just got here. We haven't seen each other since sixty-five. Don't you like my hospitality? Besides, there might be posses out there looking for us. It's best you stay here a few days until things settle down."

Stone puffed his cigarette. It looked like he had no choice.

Beau threw him the newspaper containing the railroad story. "What do you think of the transcontinental railroad, Johnny?"

"Good thing for ranchers. Get their herds to market easier."

Beau smiled sadly and shook his head. "You've become an ordinary man. You think like everybody else. Most people can't see that railroads will ruin this country. They'll bring in too many people. It'll get crowded. The beauty of this land is that nobody's here."

"What about the Indians?"

"They're not people."

"I think it's the law you're worried about, not people."

"We do what's necessary to survive. War is never pretty."

Stone leaned toward Beau. "If you want to be an outlaw—be an outlaw. But don't call yourself a soldier. And don't give me that hogwash about *guerrilla cavalry*. The only difference between your outlaw gang and any other outlaw gang is that you pretend to be something you're not."

There was silence for a few moments. Stone puffed his cigarette and glanced at the jug of whiskey. Gloria cleared the dishes off the table and left the cabin.

Stone turned to Beau. "Tell me something. Suppose, at the stagecoach holdup yesterday, one of the women had pulled a derringer. Would you've shot her?"

"Without hesitation."

"You'd kill her and take her money?"

"I'd kill anyone who stands in my way."

"Even a woman?"

"They produce the enemy soldiers of tomorrow."

"Beau, I think you've gone round the bend."

"A man with no imagination would think that."

"At least you're being consistent," Stone said. "I've got to give you that. You were always the firebreather among us, the one who wanted to go out and kill Yankees as soon as possible."

"You used to talk the same way."

"That was before I saw what war was about."

"You've seen no more war than I, and I've never changed because I had the courage of my convictions, while you were a dilettante."

Stone looked at him grimly. "I don't know what you saw, but war does nothing but get men killed. It makes some people richer and some people poorer, and the old soldiers just fade away."

"This one's not fading away," Beau said. "To hell with that. I'll fight as long as I've got fight in me." He reached for the jug, pulled out the cork, and poured whiskey into a glass, pushing it to Stone. "Have a drink."

"No thanks."

"Why not?"

"Don't feel like it."

"Got a headache? This'll make it go away."

Stone looked at the glass. He wanted desperately to drink it, but he ached all over and nearly had been beaten in a fight last night because of whiskey.

"No thanks."

"There's always been something of the moralist in you," Beau said. "Maybe you should've become a preacher. I can see you in a black suit with a white collar. You'd probably give a helluva sermon. You don't mind if I have a drink, do you?"

"Help yourself."

Beau raised the glass to his mouth. Stone felt restless and claustrophobic.

"Think I'll take a walk," he said. "Could use some exercise."

"Don't try to leave without saying good-bye, Johnny."

Stone walked to the door, his cigarette dangling out the corner of his mouth. He went outside and took a deep draught of air, and it smelled clean and pure. His head didn't feel so bad anymore. He wanted to work the kinks out of his muscles.

Gloria appeared around the corner of the house, standing in his way. "I want to talk with you," she said. "I think there's something you ought to know. He's only got one lung. So if you plan to fight him, just remember you'll be fighting a man with only one lung."

"I'm not going to fight him. Don't worry about it."

"You'd better not, if you want to get out of this camp alive. The men don't like you. You're just another turncoat as far as they're concerned. So watch your step. If anything happens to Beau, you're dead."

"You think I'm a turncoat too?"

"I don't know what I think anymore."

She turned abruptly and walked away.

Approximately five miles away, Jesse Culpepper was on his hands and knees at the shore of Rattlesnake River.

He stared directly down at the tracks he'd been following for two days, and estimated around twenty mounted men had come this way on shod horses, which meant they weren't Indians. He looked across the river and didn't see any tracks on the other side, but he'd have to go over and check.

He stood, took off his hat, and wiped his forehead with the back of his arm. He'd trailed the thief who'd stolen his wallet into this country, and then lost him. While trying to pick up his trail, Culpepper had come upon new tracks. It appeared that these riders and the thief were headed in the same direction. Culpepper intended to follow the tracks and see if they led him to the thief.

He'd taken a good look at him, in that privy back in Clarksdale. He'd been young, with curly black hair and a square face. Culpepper would know him if he saw him again here or in hell.

Culpepper climbed atop his saddle and urged his horse forward. His horse crossed the river as Culpepper looked at the cliffs around him, his Sharps rifle cradled in his arms.

When his horse reached the other side, Culpepper dismounted and studied the riverbank.

There were no tracks. That meant the riders had either gone upstream or downstream. Culpepper waded out into the river and bent over, picking up rocks from the bottom, looking for the marks of horseshoes.

Finally he found some, and picked up more rocks. It took him a half hour of systematic work before he determined that the riders had gone upstream.

Culpepper climbed onto his horse and directed it into the middle of the river. The dun plodded along, dipping its snout into the water while Culpepper scrutinized the banks on both sides, looking for tracks.

"Diane—what's bothering you? You haven't been the same since you came back from that stagecoach holdup."

The Earl of Dunwich and Lady Diane Farlington were seated in the restaurant of the Carrington Arms. Sunlight streamed through the windows, and they could see riders on the street outside.

"I wonder why the outlaws took John Stone with them?" she said.

"Obviously they knew him."

"It's hard to believe that a man like him could be mixed up with them."

"I know what you mean. He seemed to be a decent chap. But it's rather odd."

"They knew him," Diane said, "but maybe he wasn't in with them. Maybe they knew him from somewhere else. Maybe they'd crossed him, or he'd crossed them, and now they're going to kill him."

"I think you're letting your imagination run away with you, dear."

"They were a mean bunch, Paul. I never understood what fear was until I looked into their eyes."

"Have another drink."

Edward McManus entered the dining room and walked toward their table, removing his new stovepipe hat.

"The sheriff hasn't been able to find out anything about John Stone, and nobody's claimed the reward money yet." He lowered his considerable bulk into a chair. "By the way, have you heard the news about our schoolmarm friend, Priscilla Bellevue? She ran off with Bob, one of those two cowboys who ran into us on the road the other day. Strange how some women are fascinated by those fellows."

John Stone walked briskly across the valley, stomach in and chest out like a soldier, old habits come back quickly. He breathed deeply and rolled his shoulders, feeling his body come to life.

Breakfast, coffee, and the exercise had done wonders, and he felt the clouds evaporating in his mind. His face and ribs hurt, but he wasn't worried about serious damage anymore. He swore to never let himself be beaten again as he'd been beaten last night.

He walked among the cattle grazing in the valley, and they looked at him lazily. The movement energized and reminded him of the parade ground at West Point, where'd he'd marched many miles, and some of them had been at the side of Beau Talbott.

They'd been young cadets, full of romantic notions about the profession of arms, splendid in their gray and white uniforms. Stone wanted to remember that Beau Talbott, and forget the current one.

Beau had been passionate in his political beliefs when he was young, but now was a die-hard fanatic. Either that or he just plain loved war. Stone had known other soldiers who'd been unable to give it up.

There was something free about being a soldier, beyond the rules of ordinary human conduct, and something wonderful about fighting for a noble cause. If it was noble. Was there such a thing? Or was it a fight for the McManuses, the bankers?

Stone admired Beau's steadfastness, but outlaws like Beau made life unsafe for everybody. Stone wanted to lead something like a normal life, while Beau was the antithesis of normal life.

A bush in front of him stirred. Stone stopped in his tracks and whipped out his two Colts.

Ewell stepped out from behind a bush. "I wanted to thank you," he said.

Stone dropped his Colts into their holsters. "Don't mention it."

Ewell approached him, a boyish smile on his face. "I remember you when I was little, and I remember Ashley too. We were all so happy in those days, weren't we?" Ewell looked to the side. "By the way, that thing that happened in town—it'll be our own little secret, right?"

"I never saw you in town, Ewell, so don't worry."

Ewell winked. He turned and walked into the cottonwoods and oaks. In seconds he was gone.

Stone walked back toward the main cabins and saw a group of outlaws lounging about in front of the bunkhouse.

Cavanaugh was among them, his face battered and a bandage

covered his nose. Cavanaugh glared at Stone and Stone glared back. One of the men muttered something. Stone changed direction and walked toward the outlaws.

"Did I hear one of you say something?" Stone asked, looking down at them.

They sat on chairs, boxes, and the ground, and nobody replied.

"If anybody's got something to say to me, I hope he'll step forward. He's got nothing to lose, except a few inches of his hide." Stone looked at Cavanaugh. "How about you?"

Cavanaugh didn't say anything.

"I just asked you a question, mister."

"Shove your question up your ass."

Beau's voice rang out. "Hold it right there!"

Everyone looked at Beau, walking toward them from the main house, his wide black hat low over his eyes and tilted to the side.

"Johnny, I'll have to ask you to stay away from the men while you're here."

"Tell them to keep their mouths shut when I'm around."

Beau looked at his men. "Leave him alone. He'll be gone in a few days. Stay away from him."

The men grumbled, and one of them spat at the ground. They turned around and filed into the bunkhouse.

Beau placed his arm around Stone's shoulders and walked toward the house.

"You don't have to like them," Beau said. "Just keep away from them."

"Somebody ought to write an article for the *Cavalry Quarterly* about the degeneration of regular troops as guerrillas."

"They outnumbered you about twenty to one. They might've shot you if I hadn't showed up."

"I thought you said you told them to leave me alone."

"Don't provoke them."

"In other words, you're really not in command."

"Guerrilla cavalry is more loosely organized than regular units."

"What'll you do if someday they turn on you? They're a bunch of cutthroats and back-shooters if ever I saw them."

"They'll follow me as long as I can lead effectively. The Department of the Army didn't make me their commander. In a guerrilla unit, you command on your merits, and not because of the rank on your shoulders."

They came to the backyard. Hattie was hanging the wash. A row of bottles and cans were lined up on a plank suspended between two barrels.

Beau stopped and turned to Stone. "I see you're wearing two Colts. Know how to use them?"

"I wouldn't wear them if I didn't know how to use them."

"Care to have a little contest?"

"All right."

"Hattie—would you come over here for a moment?"

She dropped the clothes into the basket and walked toward them. "What you want, Mr. Beau."

"Count to three, Hattie."

"One . . . two . . ."

Stone drew on the count of three, and Beau fired, missing his target. Stone pulled his trigger a split second later, and his bottle exploded in the air.

"He beat you, Mr. Beau," Hattie said.

Beau looked at Stone and smiled. "I was faster."

"But you missed."

"Care to try again?"

"Sure."

They holstered their guns and faced the targets.

"Hattie—start counting please."

"One . . . two . . ."

Stone snapped out his gun and fired, sending a can flying into the air. Beau fired and shattered a bottle.

"He beat you, Mr. Beau."

"Hattie, I think you can go back to what you were doing."

Hattie walked toward the clothesline. Beau turned to Stone. "You're pretty fast, Johnny. How'd you get to be so fast?"

"Necessity."

"Want to try it again?"

"Mr. Colt loves his work."

"I'll throw up a rock, and when it hits the ground, fire."

Beau picked up a rock and stood beside Stone. He threw the rock in the air and went into his shooter's crouch. Both men waited, hands poised above their guns. The rock smacked into the ground and they grabbed iron. Stone was clear of his holster first, but something told him he'd better let Beau win one, because Beau was getting mad. He fired wide of the mark.

Beau drilled his can through the middle, and turned to Stone. "Your aim was off that time because you fired too soon. It's a common mistake. You should never fire before you've drawn your bead." Beau tossed the rock into the air again, and both of the men got ready. The rock bounced off a boulder, and their guns flew out of their holsters.

Stone fired first, and a tin can went rocketing through the air. Beau fired immediately afterward, and his can was launched into space also.

"Practice much?" Beau asked.

"Whenever I can."

"Maybe I should practice more. Been kind of lax lately. Want to try once more?"

"Mr. Colt never says no."

Beau took off his hat and ran his fingers through his thick black hair, and Stone detected a few gray strands near his temples. Beau licked his lips and put his hat back on.

"Ready?" he asked.

He threw the rock, went for his gun, and fired before the rock hit the ground. His bullet sent the shards of a bottle spattering through the air.

"I believe you fired before the rock hit the ground," Stone said.

"Johnny, now really."

"You mean you didn't?"

"Let's not stoop to that, Johnny. Lose like a man. How about one more?"

"Not interested."

"How come?"

Beau had a fierce gleam in his eyes, and Stone knew he'd better back off. Beau wasn't right in his mind anymore, and it wouldn't do to antagonize him.

"Okay," Stone told him. "Mr. Colt never gets enough exercise."

Beau threw the rock, and Stone slowed himself down, firing a brief interval after Beau did.

Beau hit his target, and Stone missed on purpose. Beau smiled and dropped his gun into its holster. "Guess that settles it," he said. "Can I buy you a drink?"

• • •

Culpepper turned the bend in the river, and saw the waterfall tumbling down the side of the cliff with a mighty roar.

He'd heard the waterfall for the past two hours and had been moving ever closer to it. Now it was straight ahead, sending a mist into the rainbow overhead. The bright sun bathed the scene in a golden glow.

"What the hell's going on here?" Culpepper muttered. He looked backward and forward and tried to figure it out. It appeared that the riders rode directly into the waterfall, but how could that be?

He grit his teeth and sucked wind. There was only one thing to do. He had to get into the water again.

He rode the dun onto the riverbank, picketed it, and loosed the two cinches on the saddle. Then he stripped off his shirt and waded into the water. He bent over, picked up rocks, and examined them for horseshoe marks.

The riders had come this way, according to the scarred rocks. Culpepper followed them forward, moving closer to the waterfall, lifting rocks up from the river bottom and peering at them.

Finally he came to the foot of the waterfall, and its mist rose around him, tickled his nostrils. He thought about diving into the cascades, but worried he might split his skull against the cliff. *Maybe I can get around it.*

He moved to the side, as his horse watched him curiously, pricking up its ears. Culpepper came to the edge of the water-fall and tried to look behind it, but the water flowed close to the rocks, and he couldn't see anything.

Culpepper scratched his head. He walked back to his horse, took out his tobacco, rolled a cigarette, and lit it. Then he looked back at the waterfall.

The riders evidently had ridden directly through it. That's what the trail said, and the trail didn't lie.

Culpepper had tracked Indians for the Fifth Cavalry, and thought he knew all the tricks of the game, but this was a new one. There was only one thing to do: follow the trail through the waterfall.

He kneeled and smoked the cigarette down to a butt, then tossed it into the river. Standing, he waded in again and walked toward the waterfall, entering the mists.

He gazed at the foaming wall of water in front of him, and the trail said the riders went right through. If they'd gone right through, so could he.

He took a deep breath and dived into the cascading white water, holding his hands out so they'd hit rock before his head did.

Tons of water pounded him, and then he was on the other side, blinking his eyes. He looked down the tunnel and saw the light.

"I'll be a son of a bitch!"

Stone sat at the kitchen table, staring at the jug of whiskey.

Beau was talking about General Ulysses S. Grant. "Never in history has a commander squandered men the way he did. Why, he had no respect for human life at all. He just threw troops at us with no strategic skill and no subtlety. The man should've been a butcher, but instead he was commander in chief of the Yankee Army. Shows you what they were all about."

Stone ate roast pork and mashed potatoes. The whiskey urge was on him now. Every fiber in his body yearned to feel that mellow glow. Beau's voice droned in his ears.

"What do you think of Grant as a commander, Johnny?"

"I'm not interested in fighting the war anymore."

"I'd be interested to hear your opinion."

"Don't have one."

"Have you gone numb between your ears, Johnny?"

"Guess so, Beau."

"A commander learns to wage war in the future by studying the great battles of the past."

Stone didn't reply. Beau noticed him looking at the jug.

"Have a drink," Beau said, pushing the jug toward him.

"No thanks."

"Don't like my whiskey?"

"It's good whiskey, Beau, but I'd like to stop drinking so much."

Beau poured himself a glass. "A man has to control his appetites. If he can't control himself, how can he expect to control others?" He raised the glass to his lips. "I have no trouble controlling myself. It's all a matter of will."

"So I've noticed," Stone said. "You just drink all the time."

Gloria couldn't stifle a laugh. Beau looked coldly at her. There was a knock on the door.

"Come in!" Beau said.

The door opened and Chance Stevens stepped into the cabin. He looked at Stone, and Stone got to his feet.

"What're you doin' here?" Chance asked Stone.

"He's an old friend of mine," Beau replied. "How do you two know each other?"

"Met him in Clarksdale. Owes me a game of cards." He looked at Stone. "How long you stayin'?"

"Couple more days."

"How's about having that game of cards you promised me, afore you leave?"

"Don't have any money."

"What happened to it?"

Stone looked at Beau. "He stole it."

Beau widened his eyes, then burst into laughter. "I haven't given you back your money, Johnny?"

"No you haven't, Beau."

"Guess I forgot. How much was it?"

"I had about forty dollars on me, and the stagecoach line owed another ten or eleven."

"I'll get it for you right after lunch. You should've said something. I don't want your money."

The door swung open, and Stone saw Dorchester, the hunchback cowboy, standing there in his big hat. Dorchester looked at Stone, drew back his lips, and reached for his gun, but Stone's guns already were moving into action. Gloria screamed, Veronica stared into space, and everyone dived toward the floor.

The room filled with explosions of gunfire, and acrid smoke billowed in the air. The hunchback staggered to the side, two red splotches on his dirty white shirt. He dropped his gun, stared at Stone, and then his eyes rolled up into his head. His knees buckled and he dropped to the floor.

Stone holstered his gun and reached for the jug of whiskey. He poured some into a glass and downed it.

Beau picked himself up off the floor. "What the hell was that all about?"

Stone poured himself another glass of whiskey. "I met the gentleman in Clarksdale. He tried to shoot me in the back."

Chance turned to Stone. "So it was you he had the run-in with."

Beau walked toward Dorchester and kneeled beside his bleeding corpse. "Poor little freak."

Veronica's hands trembled slightly. "I'm not feeling well. Johnny, would you see me to my room?"

Stone stood and extended his arm. Veronica took it, and they walked side by side out of the kitchen.

"Sometimes I get dizzy spells," Veronica said. "Must be something in the air."

"Must be."

"Ashley's been mean lately. Why hasn't he called?"

"Maybe he'll drop by tonight."

"Do you really think he might?"

"Lie down and rest. You'll feel better after a while."

"Daddy was saying the other day that somebody ought to shoot Mr. Lincoln. What do you think of that, Johnny?"

"Just lie down."

"A body hardly knows what to think anymore. Why can't everything be nice like it was?"

She lay on the bed and closed her eyes. Stone looked down at her, and she smelled like old clothes. He needed another drink.

He walked back to the kitchen. Two of Beau's men were carrying Dorchester's body outside. Hattie mopped up the blood. Stone sat at the table and reached for the jug.

"How is she?" Beau asked Stone.

"Seems to be okay."

"I see you're drinking again."

Stone filled the glass and poured it down his throat. His right hand was shaking slightly.

Chance sat at the table. Gloria and Ewell returned to their seats. Everyone stared at the food, but nobody ate.

"That was a close call," Beau said to Stone. "Dorchester was a fast little skunk. You were lucky."

Stone pushed the jug away. He knew if he continued drinking, he'd be lying on the floor.

"What did you do to Dorchester?" asked Talbott.

"I bumped into him by mistake on the street, and he was going to kill me for it. Another of your gallant idealists, huh, Beau?"

"Dorchester always had a short fuse." He turned to Chance. "Any interesting news?"

Chance leaned his elbows on the table. "Nine thousand dollars in gold is leaving for San Francisco by stage on the first of the month. There'll be two guards."

Beau gazed into the middle distance. "Get Cavanaugh and Shattuck in here."

Hattie cleared off the table. Stone poured himself another glass of whiskey and stepped back out of the way. *This is my last one*, he said to himself.

Beau took a rolled map down from a shelf and spread it out on the table. The door opened and Cavanaugh entered, followed by a man with buckteeth and no discernible chin. They gathered around the table.

Beau told the newcomers about the gold shipment, and they planned the robbery. Stone sat on a wooden chair against the far wall and watched.

It was like a commanding officer and his staff developing the strategy for battle. Stone rolled a cigarette and was impressed by how smoothly the various players interacted.

Beau was firmly in charge, and the others obviously respected him. He had the aura of command about him, and looked very much like the enthusiastic young officer who'd commanded Troop D of the old Hampton Brigade.

Chance evidently was the spy who obtained raw information, and Napoleon said one good spy in the right place was worth an army in the field.

Cavanaugh was first sergeant, in charge of fundamental operations. Gloria was the medical corps. Shattuck's responsibility was supply. And Ewell was the executive officer to whom nobody paid any real attention.

There was a knock on the door. Beau looked up from the map table. "Come in."

The door opened, and one of the outlaws stood there. "We caught us an intruder."

Beau put on his hat and went outside. The others followed, and Stone placed the jug of whiskey on the table before he left the kitchen.

He saw the outlaws gathered in front of the cabin, and two of them were holding the bound arms of a man Stone recognized immediately.

It was Jesse Culpepper, hatless, with a few wheat-straw strands of hair lying on his mostly bald head. His hands were tied behind his back and his face was sunburned.

Beau sauntered toward him. "Who the hell are you?"

"My name's Jesse Culpepper, and I'm trackin' the man who stole my wallet from the pisshouse in Clarksdale."

The outlaws laughed, and even Beau cracked a smile. An expression of hope came over Culpepper's face, as if it were all a big joke and nothing to worry about.

"How'd you find this place?"

"Jest follered yer tracks."

"From where?"

Culpepper described how he'd tracked the thief out of town and run into the sign of a larger group of riders heading in the same direction.

"You must be a great tracker, Mr. Culpepper."

"Used to scout for the Fifth Cavalry."

"Came right through the waterfall, huh?"

"Don't mean no trouble. Jest huntin' fer the man what stole my wallet." Culpepper looked around at the outlaws. "Don't see him here, though."

"What did he look like?"

"About sixteen years old, black curly hair, kind of good-lookin' but with the heart of a polecat."

Beau's face became clouded, and he spun around. "Where's Ewell?"

"He's not here," Cavanaugh said.

"Take some men and get him!"

Cavanaugh and four outlaws walked toward Ewell's cabin. Beau turned back to Culpepper, who'd just recognized Stone in the crowd.

"What're you doin' here?" Culpepper asked.

"Just another prisoner of war," Stone said.

Culpepper turned to Beau. "He was standin' on the street when that polecat ran by."

Beau looked at Stone. "You saw the person who took this man's wallet?"

"It was dark."

Jesse Culpepper shook his head. "Weren't that dark," he said bitterly.

"Was it Ewell?" Beau asked Stone.

A horrible screech rent the air, and everyone looked in the direction of Ewell's cabin. Cavanaugh and another outlaw were carrying Ewell outside, and he kicked and struggled. His hat had fallen off his head, showing his hair.

"I do believe that's him," Culpepper said.

Cavanaugh and the other outlaw carried Ewell into the gathering and let him go. Ewell angrily readjusted his clothes, averting his gaze from Culpepper.

"That's the man," Culpepper said, pointing at Ewell.

Ewell's face drained of color as he looked at Beau. Their eyes met, and the muscle in Beau's jaw was working. Then Beau turned to Culpepper and drew his pistol.

"Don't do it!" Stone said.

Beau ignored him and drew a bead on Culpepper, who closed his eyes and grit his teeth. Stone yanked out his Colt and fired. Beau's gun flew out of his hand.

A billow of gunsmoke rose into the air, and Stone looked around. Every outlaw had his gun trained on him. Stone dropped his gun back into his holster. Beau shook the sting out of his hand, walked a few steps, bent over, and picked up his gun, wiping off the dust.

Stone said, "You can't just shoot him in cold blood!"

"Stay out of this, Johnny!"

"He's an innocent man!"

"Nobody's innocent . . . not you, not me, and not this nosy son of a bitch!"

Beau fired his pistol, and Culpepper staggered, raising his hands to his chest. His legs gave out and he fell to the ground. Beau holstered his gun, rushed at Ewell, and grabbed the front of his shirt with one hand, slapping him repeatedly with the other.

"You cheap little thief!" Beau hollered as Ewell cringed before him. "You petty little bastard! Don't you ever disgrace your family like that again!"

Ewell whimpered as he fell to the ground, and Beau kept slapping him, his insults becoming indecipherable in his anger. Ewell sank lower with each blow, cowering beneath the lash of Beau's hand.

6

STONE SPENT THE afternoon in the woods near the outlaw hideout. He walked, smoked cigarettes, sat on rocks, and watched meandering little streams.

He wanted to get out of the canyon and back to the real world. He felt as if he were in a snake pit. Beau had become deranged, his men were killers, and everything was deadly.

He'd been shocked by how cold-bloodedly Beau had shot Culpepper. Beau never hesitated or experienced a moment of doubt. He'd killed Culpepper the way he'd swat a fly. Beau was even further over the edge than Stone had thought.

Stone knew he'd have to be careful with Beau. There'd be no more arguing, no confrontations. He'd have to be calm and cool, and work toward getting out of the camp peacefully. If he had to shoot his way out, he'd do it, but he'd rather take the easier way.

Toward late afternoon he walked back to the cabins. As he emerged from the sage, he saw Beau stripped to the waist, chopping wood with a long axe.

Beau's upper body was pale, and as Stone drew closer, he saw the ugly scar on Beau's left breast. It looked as though the bones had caved in behind the scar.

Beau looked up as Stone approached, then resumed chopping wood. Stone stood a few feet to the side and rolled a cigarette.

117

The skin on Beau's torso was flaccid, but when he poised himself to strike the wood, his striated muscles stood out beneath the surface. He gave the impression of strength and ill health at the same time. Raising the axe in the air, he brought it down swiftly and split the round of wood in half.

Stone lit the cigarette, and Beau wiped his forehead with the palm of his hand. "Guess you're anxious to get moving along."

"You might say that."

"You can leave in the morning, if you like."

"Sounds good to me."

"Your money's on the table in the kitchen."

Stone walked toward the house and entered the kitchen. Hattie stood at the stove, stirring a pot, and the fragrance of baking bread was in the air. He saw the stacks of coins on the table. Sitting in front of them, he tallied them up. The total was fifty dollars.

He puffed his cigarette. His eyes fell on the jug of whiskey in the middle of the table. He'd known it was there, calling out to him as he counted the money, but he'd ignored it.

Now it stared him in the face, and he wanted a drink to steady him. Not that he felt that unsteady, but a good shot of whiskey could make a man even more steady, although after a while it would make him into a stumbling fool.

He pushed the jug away. The door opened and Chance walked into the kitchen, a wide smile on his face. "Heard you got paid back," he said. "How's about that game of cards?"

"Not in the mood."

"If you're leavin' in the mornin', this'll be our last opportunity to see who's the better man."

"Not interested."

Chance sat opposite him at the table and removed his hat. His head looked like a grinning skull. "Afraid to lose?"

"Don't feel like playing cards."

"Stakes don't have to be high."

"Maybe later."

"You should never wait until later, because sometimes later never comes." He whipped out a deck of cards. "What's yer game? Not afraid are you? Let's play somethin' simple, like seven-card stud."

"Last time you played poker, you lost your shirt."

"This time you'll lose yours."

"Where'd you meet Beau?"

"In the hospital after the war."

"What did you do before the war?"

"Just what I'm doin' now." Chance gave the deck a fancy shuffle and dealt the cards. "Been a gamblin' man since I was sixteen. Gambled my way all over this country. You'd be surprised, the amount of information a man can pick up in saloons."

"Chance, I believe you dealt that last one off the bottom."

Chance froze, the deck of cards poised in his hand. "You'd better be careful when you say that." He dropped the cards to the table and got to his feet. "Are you callin' me a cheater?"

Stone remained seated, and looked up at Chance calmly. "I'm only saying I saw you deal that ace of clubs off the bottom."

Chance winked. "How d'ya 'spect me to make money gamblin' if'n I don't cheat?" He sat down and reached for the jug. "You got good eyes. People generally don't catch me."

Chance sipped some whiskey and Beau entered the kitchen. "Find something to do," he said to Chance.

Chance gulped down his glass of whiskey and stood, hitching up his belt. Then he walked in long strides toward the door. Beau sat at the table and reached for the jug.

"You'd better sleep here in the main house tonight," Beau said. "You'll get your throat cut if you sleep in the bunkhouse. The men are riled up."

"Doesn't take much to rile that bunch, I don't imagine."

"They're good soldiers, and that's all that matters."

"Your intelligence officer just tried to cheat me at cards."

"He brings me critical information. He's effective."

"Where's the honor in associating with a bunch of back-stabbers, dry-gulchers, and petty cheats?"

"A commander must use the material at hand. A commander must make hard decisions. I guess you think I shouldn't've shot that fool who blundered into here today, but I couldn't let him go. He might've ruined my entire operation. This isn't a carefree little hunt in the country, as in the old days, Johnny. This is war."

"Don't tell me about war. I've seen a fair amount myself. The main difference between you and me is you love it and

I don't. You're not happy unless there's death and destruction taking place. You love the smell of blood."

"You always take the common view, because you have a common mind. You had more imagination when you were younger."

"I was dumber when I was young. Let's talk about reality. I don't own a horse. How'm I going to get out of here in the morning if I don't have a horse, or were you planning to get rid of me the way you got rid of Jesse Culpepper?"

"I'll give you a horse. It's the least I can do for my old boyhood friend."

"Is it a stolen horse?"

"All our horses are stolen." Beau looked askance at Stone. "Wish we could be like the old days."

"Beau, the owlhoot trail isn't going to get you anything except a bullet or the noose."

It fell silent in the cabin, and Stone thought maybe he'd gone too far, but the whiskey had loosened his tongue. *That's the trouble with this damned stuff. Makes you say what you shouldn't.*

Beau gazed thoughtfully at him. "You want to talk about reality?" he asked. "Okay, here's some reality for you. You're flat on your ass broke, and how're you going to find Marie in this country without some money in your pocket? You ride with me, Johnny, and you'll have money enough to hire a dozen Pinkerton men to look for her. That's the only way you'll find her, with money, *dinero*, and money's what I know how to get."

Stone realized what Beau said made sense. *What've I got to show for my trouble—nothing!* The Pinkerton men could find anybody. If he had money, he could have Marie, and Beau sure knew all about getting money.

He'd like to be pals with Beau as in the old days, and not be alone anymore. The frontier sure got desolate sometimes. He could stop drifting, and the Pinkerton men would find Marie.

All he'd have to do was hold up stagecoaches and banks, and one day a poor fool with a snootful of bad whiskey would draw on him, and Stone would have to shoot him, for a handful of dollars.

Stone shook his head slowly. "Can't do it."

Beau sighed. "I know you can't, you poor son of a bitch. You're bolted to that saddle of yours, and you can't get out of it."

"What about you, Beau? You've got your *dinero*, but that's all you've got. How'd you like to wake up in the morning with your head clear, and nobody's after your ass, you don't owe anything to anybody, and nobody's going to shoot you in the back? It's a nice feeling to be free, Beau. It's not living in a palace or even your old mansion back in South Carolina, but there's something to it that's sweet and fine."

Stone could see that Beau was thinking about it, but then Beau said grimly; "I can't drink from that stream, Johnny. I already rode through it on my horse, and raised a lot of mud, which is never going to settle in my life, and sometimes I think I don't have much longer to go anyway, so I guess it doesn't matter much either way."

Stone grinned. "You're too mean to die, Beau. I wouldn't worry about that if I were you."

Beau sipped some whiskey. "Too bad about what happened to us," he said. "We used to be such good friends, but now we don't even speak the same language."

Ewell sat in his little cabin, looking at the picture of his mother above the fireplace.

His only furniture was a bed, chair, and desk. The desk had a book on it and an inkwell. Gloria had been trying to teach Ewell how to read and write, but Ewell hadn't been a good pupil. He'd rather be hunting in the woods, or going to town and stealing wallets.

The main thing he liked in town was the prostitutes. He spent all his money on them, and had a real good time. One of them tied him to a bed once and whipped his bottom. It was exciting stuff.

But now Beau would never let him go to town again.

It had been humiliating the way Beau slapped him in front of the others that afternoon. Ewell had bruises all over his face. His momma wouldn't let Beau do that to him, if she were alive.

He looked up at her picture and wished she was there. She died during the war, after the Yankees burned the plantation. Ewell had been twelve at the time.

His hero always had been Beau, and his secondary heroes were John Stone and Ashley Tredegar. They were the three musketeers, in his youthful imagination, always riding horses, splendid in their uniforms.

They'd treated him like a child, and even now Beau looked down on him as if he were a moron. Ewell felt as if something were wrong with him, and his life were split in two. One half had been wonderful, and the last half, since the war, a nightmare.

He wanted to be free of his mean brother and crazy sister, and all the brutes in the gang who laughed at him behind his back. He wanted to have his own money and travel around like the drifters he saw in Clarksdale and other towns.

He had no remorse about the money he'd stolen from Jesse Culpepper. As far as Ewell was concerned, he was at war with the world, and anything went. That's what he'd learned from Beau, and couldn't understand why Beau was mad at him. What was the difference between stealing a man's wallet in a pisshouse, or taking it from him in a stagecoach holdup?

Beau mystified him. He could never predict what Beau would do next. Like at the holdup, when Beau brought John Stone home.

Ewell hadn't recognized John Stone when he'd first seen him. Stone had gotten a lot bigger and older. Looked awful hard. The old John Stone from South Carolina had been happy-go-lucky, quite unlike this galoot with the two guns and eyes that ran right through you.

It was time for supper, and Ewell dreaded it. Everyone had seen him get slapped around by Beau, and he'd feel like a shithouse rat. That's the way they always treated him, and sometimes he suspected they were right, and he really was a shithouse rat.

I've got to get away from them. He arose, put on his hat, and walked outside. In order to get to Beau's cabin, he had to pass the bunkhouse, and a bunch of men were outside, sitting around and smoking, shooting the breeze.

Ewell pulled his hat low onto his head until it covered his eyebrows. He walked toward Beau's cabin with resolute steps.

One of them burped. Another muttered something. "The pisshouse kid," said a third.

They all burst into laughter, and Ewell's ears turned red. If you rob a man on the open road, it's all right, but if you rob a man in a pisshouse, it's not all right. Ewell tried to figure out the big difference.

He came to the main building and opened the door. Stone sat in a corner, reading an old newspaper. Beau and Gloria were at the table, and Beau had a glass in his hand. Hattie worked at the stove. Nobody said anything to him.

Ewell hung up his hat and sat at the table. He could feel the pressure of the afternoon against his skin. Everybody knew he was the pisshouse kid.

He wished he could sit at a table in a saloon where no one knew him. Then he could feel like a man among men, and there wouldn't be the pressure against his skin. And he'd have plenty of money: drunks with fat wallets, old ladies who lived alone, and he could try the pisshouse trick in every town. Maybe he could even get together a gang.

Veronica entered the room, a ragged yellow ribbon in her hair. "Time to eat?"

"A few more minutes," said Hattie at the stove.

"I had the most wonderful afternoon," Veronica said, sitting pertly on the edge of a chair. "Ashley and I went to a little bookstore, and we found a beautifully illustrated edition of Mr. William Shakespeare's *Macbeth*. He insisted I have it, and bought it for me. Ashley's so generous, isn't he? And he recited, from memory, those wonderful lines: *'Life's but a walking shadow, a poor player that frets and struts his hour upon the stage and then is heard no more: it is a tale told by an idiot, full of sound and fury, signifying nothing.'"*

"Time to eat," Hattie said, placing a roast-beef platter in the middle of the table.

They ate in silence, except for Veronica's prattling about Ashley. Everybody was used to it and nobody paid any attention, as if she were a natural form of noise, like a woodpecker or the sound of crickets.

Stone knew it was his last supper with the Talbotts. He looked across the table at Beau, and saw that Beau was looking at him.

"I was just remembering something, Johnny," Beau said, "that night you, Ashley, and I went AWOL from the Point and took the ferry down to New York City." A smile came over Beau's face. "What a night that was. We drank our way across town, in every cesspool of sin on the island, and in many of the finest drinking establishments also. People bought us liquor wherever we went, because we were in uniform and they knew we were cadets. We spent the night in some woods farther uptown. I tell you, Johnny, those were the days."

"As I recall, you threw up all over your uniform."

"I wasn't too used to drinking in those days."

"And we nearly got court-martialed when we got back."

"Well," said Beau, "fortunately Custer was on guard, and he let us through the gate." Beau shook his head slowly. "Custer never had a brain in his head, yet rose to high command. Goes to show you what the Yankee Army is all about. What do you think about the Indian situation. Johnny?"

"Most of their hard-liners will get killed, and the rest will knuckle under."

"Don't have much of a chance, do they? But I admire the ones who fight back. Can't respect the ones that go onto the reservation. They're not worth the salt in their hay." Beau looked at Stone. "I guess that's what you've become in my eyes, Johnny. This white man's equivalent of a reservation Indian."

"Think what you like."

"I'm disappointed in you."

"That knife cuts both ways."

"I liked the old days better. That's the way I want to remember you."

"The old days're gone. I think it's time you got that through your head."

"You want me to come onto the reservation with you, Johnny? You won't find me there. I'm not a reservation Indian."

"Neither am I."

"If you're not a reservation Indian, what are you?"

"A future cattleman, I hope."

"What do you know about cattle?"

"It's honest."

"Your implication is I'm not honest."

Stone looked at him unswervingly. "You're a bandit and a cold-blooded killer, but that's all right, that's your life. And who knows—maybe you really are a great guerrilla commander. Either way, I don't give a damn. I'm going to Texas."

Beau poured whiskey into his glass. "Let's have one last toast together, can we?"

"I've stopped drinking."

"Since when?"

"Last hour or two."

Beau pushed a glass toward him. "We'll probably never see each other again, Johnny. We ought to have a last toast. If we meet again, we shall smile. If not, this parting is well-made."

Beau reached for the glass. He filled it and waited for the others to fill theirs. Beau looked sloshed on the other side of the table. They raised their glasses in the air.

"To all the men in gray," Beau said, "wherever they may be. May the good Lord protect them and keep them, because they were all brave hearts."

They touched glasses, and Stone drained his every drop. He lowered his glass to the table and looked at the jug. Now that he'd had one drink, another wouldn't hurt. It'd help the dinner go down easier. Tomorrow he could stop drinking.

He reached for the glass again.

Stone lay sprawled in drunken slumber on the sofa in the living room, wheezing through his nostrils. The blanket had fallen off him and his feet hung over the floor, because his body was too long for the sofa. The window was open and the fragrance of the sage blew over him.

He heard a sound, and his mind stirred. Footsteps approached, and he opened one eye.

It was Veronica, wearing a long white nightgown, approaching with one finger in front of her lips. "Sssshhhhh," she said. "It's me."

Stone sat up on the sofa and rubbed his eyes. She dropped down next to him and turned in his direction.

"I was quiet," she said. "Daddy would spank me if he knew I was here, Ashley. But I couldn't stay away."

The cosmetics were gone from her face, and in the darkness she looked as she'd been before the war.

"I'm not Ashley," he said hoarsely.

She touched his cheek. "Oh, Ashley, you're always playing with me. Sometimes I think you don't love me anymore. You do still love me, don't you?"

"I'm John Stone."

"If you think you're being funny, you're wrong. Hold me in your arms, Ashley. I want to feel your body against mine."

She reached toward him, and he held her wrists. "Wake up, Veronica. Snap out of it."

"I think you're being just horrid to toy with me this way when you know how much I love you, Ashley. Haven't I already proved to you how much I love you?"

They heard Beau's voice in the doorway. "Go to bed, Veronica."

An expression of alarm came over her face. "Beau—what are you doing here!"

Beau took her arm and gently raised her from the sofa. "Come to bed, dear."

He led her to her bedroom, disappearing into the darkness. Stone rolled himself a cigarette in the darkness and lit it. After a brief interval, Beau came out of the bedroom and closed the door softly.

"Can I have a word with you in the kitchen, Johnny?"

Stone pulled on his boots and followed Beau into the kitchen. Beau lit the lamp on the table and reached for the jug.

"Have a seat."

Stone dropped onto a chair and puffed his cigarette. Beau poured two glasses of whiskey and pushed one toward Stone.

"I appreciate what you just did, Johnny. Another man would've taken advantage of her, but not you. You're still a man of honor—I can see that now. I could trust you with my sister or anything else that was dear to me, and know you'd do the right thing. Times change and people get older, but it's nice to know some things remain the same." Beau sipped his whiskey, looked into the glass, then raised his eyes to Stone. "We'll probably never see each other again, Johnny, and I'd like to tell you something. I know what you think of me, and sometimes, to tell you the truth, I don't know what to think of myself.

"Many a night I've sat here, looking out over that valley, and I've said to myself: What happened to glory, what happened to honor, how in hell did I end up here? You think I haven't had doubts? Sure I have. I've said to myself: Beau Talbott, you're the lowest of the low, you're the scum of the earth, the kind of man who belongs behind bars. And I think of my father, if he could look down and see me, he'd say to himself, that's no son of mine."

Stone looked at Beau, and the features of Beau's face were uneven, as if they were falling apart. "Don't be too hard on yourself, Beau," he said softly. "I know things didn't turn out the way we wanted. The sun beats down—it burns all of us. I've had my thoughts too. Do you think I wanted to lose the war? Do you think I like riding around alone, drifting from here to there, always broke, nobody cares about me, and all the men I commanded are wandering around just like me, all of us with nothing, while the goddamned politicians who sent us to war are richer than ever—you think I like that? Why couldn't the glory have been ours, Beau? Why couldn't it have been? Many times I've dreamed and seen us with the flag of victory waving over us, and sometimes I think I'll make my own little victory any way I have to, any way I can. I've thought of robbing stagecoaches myself, and a bank, and a whole lot more, but I didn't do it, and God only knows why."

Beau laughed bitterly. "So here we are," he said, "a couple of southern gentlemen hiding from the world. Johnny, it's hard to believe. But you know, I can't change now. I've gone too far into blood to change. I've waded all the way in, and I'm going clear through to the other side. And I guess it doesn't matter how much blood I wade in, because that's how the cards turned up for me, you understand that. I can't let anything get in my way. Nor anyone."

"I understand," said John Stone. "I understand better than you think."

"Thanks for that, Johnny. Let me drink to your health one last time. May you find whatever you're looking for, and may the good Lord bless and keep you."

They touched glasses and drank. Stone felt the burning liquid glide over his tongue and down his throat. He refilled the glasses.

"Let me drink to you, Beau. May the good Lord give you peace."

They touched glasses again. Beau pushed his empty glass forward and banged the cork into the jug with the heel of his hand.

"I imagine you'll want to leave early," Beau said. "I've picked out a good horse for you, and given orders that it be saddled and ready at dawn. You'll have a canteen and provisions in the saddlebags. If you maintain a steady pace, you should be in Clarksdale by midnight. I probably won't be awake when you get up, so I guess this is it."

Both men stood and moved toward each other. They shook hands firmly, looking into each other's eyes.

"I wish you could see your way to riding with us, Johnny." Beau cocked his head to one side and said thoughtfully: "We're made differently, I guess. Probably always were, only we never realized it till now. Well, happy trails to you. Maybe we'll meet again someday in the other world."

Beau released Stone's hand and blew out the lamp, plunging the room into darkness. He turned and walked away, closing the door behind him. Stone stared at the door for a few minutes, then arose and trudged to the sofa, dropping down, lying with his eyes open for a while, staring at the ceiling.

And the flaming sword of Orion shone over the two officers huddled in their hideout in the night, and over how many more like them scattered like tumbleweed to the winds, lost and desperate, while the cold stars twinkled down from far, far off. The gods smile, and young men die.

It was dark in Ewell's cabin as he put on his hat. He threw the saddlebags over his shoulder and walked out the door.

The sky was aglow with stars, and the valley stretched out before him. He knew there'd be a guard at the entrance to the valley, but Ewell came and went all the time, and nobody ever stopped him.

He walked toward the stable, the saddlebags over his shoulder. He intended to ride hard and reach Clarksdale by noon. He knew the shortcuts and if his horse got tired, he'd steal another one.

He entered the stable and found his horse, a grulla. "Hello, Dan," he said. "We're goin' for a little ride, and we ain't never comin' back."

He threw the blanket on the horse, then placed the saddle atop it. Soon he'd be free, with no one to tell him what to say or do again, and people would treat him with respect for a change.

He climbed onto the horse and rode out of the barn, heading toward the waterfall. He never once looked back at his home as the horse paced across the valley. He thought of the girls at the Crystal Palace, and smiled. Tomorrow he'd spend the night with one of them, instead of with a bunch of brutish old war veterans and his crazy sister.

He saw the guard on the cliff, waved to him, and entered the tunnel.

The roaring and hissing of the waterfall struck his ears, and moisture from the ceiling of the cave dripped onto his hat. The waterfall came closer and the grulla shied back a bit, but Ewell gave him the spurs, and the horse advanced into the rushing wall of water.

The waterfall poured onto Ewell, drenching him to his skin and running down his legs into his boots. He held on to his hat, and the horse continued walking. They came out the other side and heard a new sound, the trickling of Rattlesnake River.

Nobody'd ever better lay a hand on me again, Ewell thought as he recalled how Beau had slapped him in front of the men. *I'll kill anybody who tries.*

Ewell spat some water out of his mouth as the horse walked downstream, heading toward Clarksdale.

7

THE DAWN LIGHT shone on four biscuits on a dish in the center of the table. Beside them was a scrawled note:

To Johnny

From Hattie

Stone stuffed the biscuits into his saddlebags and went outside. The horse was tied to the hitching post as Beau had said. It was a sorrel, and pawed the earth as if it were raring to go. The sun lay beneath the mountaintop on the east side of the valley, radiating light into the sky.

Stone walked toward the sorrel and saw a bag of provisions hanging from the pommel of the saddle. A blanket roll was behind the saddle.

Stone placed his foot in the stirrup and raised himself up, swinging his leg over the saddle and settling in. A light was on in the bunkhouse, and smoke trailed from the chimney. Stone urged the horse toward the tunnel, and cattle grazing nearby munched grass as they watched him pass.

Stone rolled a cigarette as he rocked back and forth in the saddle. He lit it, inhaled some smoke, and turned around, looking back to the part of the main building where Beau lived.

Stone thought he saw a face in the window, but then it disappeared and Stone wondered if he'd imagined it. It had looked like Beau's face, but at that distance it was difficult to be sure.

At one o'clock in the afternoon, Ewell rode into Clarksdale. The big wide street was crowded with horses and wagons, and the sidewalks were full of people.

Ewell looked around him and smiled. Nobody knew him, and he could start a new life. A woman was bent over on the sidewalk, looking at merchandise in a store window, and Ewell admired her hindquarters. He had a hundred dollars with him, and thought he'd go immediately to the Crystal Palace.

He saw the sign: CLARKSDALE STABLES, and rode his horse toward the doorway. A poster was nailed to the wall, but he didn't pay any attention to it.

A man with a white mustache walked up to him. "Third stall on the left," he said. "The boy'll bring some hay."

Ewell dismounted and walked the horse into the stall, removing the saddle and blanket. He patted the horse on his rear haunch and walked outside.

He came to the poster again, and this time looked at it.

$1000 REWARD

Ewell couldn't read well, but squinted his eyes and tried to understand what the reward was for. He formed the letters slowly with his lips, and his eyes widened like saucers when he realized that the reward would be paid for information leading to the rescue of Captain John Stone, formerly of the Confederate Cavalry Corps!

Ewell took a step backward, amazed by what he'd read. *One thousand dollars!*

That was a tremendous amount of money. It could take him all the way to San Francisco, and he could live like a king. But then he realized what he'd have to do to get the money. He'd have to tell where the hideout was.

He stared at the sign as people walked by. It'd be so easy to get the money, but he couldn't betray Beau. He didn't like Beau anymore, but they were still brothers, still family. You didn't betray family.

Ewell shrugged, hitched his thumbs in his gunbelt, and walked toward the Crystal Palace. He wore a brown leather vest and a wide-brimmed hat with a low flat crown. Nobody paid any attention to him on the sidewalk, and that was just the way he wanted it. It was almost as if he were invisible.

He came to the Crystal Palace, a two-story building near the saloon district. The red lamps on either side of the door were on, and he climbed the stairs.

The door was opened by two cowboys with puffy faces and bleary eyes. They stumbled outside, and Ewell walked into the parlor. It had red wallpaper and a crystal chandelier overhead. He dropped onto a chair and rolled a cigarette, running his wet tongue along the gummed seam.

He was still thinking about the one thousand dollars. It was a tremendous amount of money, a small fortune. He'd always wondered what San Francisco was like. *Lots of rich people to rob*.

"You here again?" asked a female voice.

He looked up and saw Rebecca, his favorite whore. She was sixteen, with pale blond hair and blue eyes, wearing a pink gown with a red ribbon around her waist.

She plopped herself down on his lap, wiggled a few times, and draped her arms around his neck. "Bet I know what you want," she said with a laugh. Bringing her lips close to his ear, she whispered, "Wanna wear my pantaloons?"

His face turned red. "Shut up."

"Well, do you?"

"Let's go upstairs."

"You're gonna haveta take a bath afore we do anythin'. Hate to tell you what you smell like."

He pinched her bottom. "Will you come into the tub with me?"

She tweaked his nose. "You're a naughty little boy."

"I'm not a little boy. I'm a man."

They went to her room, and the curtains were imprinted with a pretty floral pattern. He opened the closet and looked at her clothes.

"Git out of there," she said. "You got to take a bath first. I'll tell the maid to bring the water."

She left the room, and he sat on a chair. The room smelled like perfume, and was so much nicer than his little cabin in Rattlesnake Canyon. He wasn't worried that somebody would laugh at him, and Beau would never humiliate him again.

After a while Rebecca returned to the room. "Water'll be right up," she said. "You kin start takin' yer clothes off, or would you rather I did it for you?"

"You do it," he said.

She walked toward him with a saucy smile on her lips and unbuttoned his shirt. "Haven't seen you for a while," she said. "Miss me?"

"All the time."

"You're lucky I'm workin' this afternoon. Usually I work nights. What brings you to town today?"

"I come to say good-bye to you," he told her. "I'm a-goin' to San Francisco."

"Where'd you get the money to go to San Francisco?" she asked skeptically.

"Never you mind."

She nuzzled his ear, and he felt thrills up his back. "I've always wanted to go to San Francisco," she said. "Can I come with you?"

No horses were tied to the hitching rail in front of the shack in Deadman's Flats. No stagecoach was parked in the yard, and no cowboys were passing through.

Stone climbed down from his saddle and tied the sorrel to the rail. Pushing his hat to the back of his head, he pulled off his black gloves as he walked to the door.

He'd been on the trail since he left Rattlesnake Canyon, and he was hungry. He had some hardtack in the saddlebags, but didn't want to eat it if he didn't have to.

Stone walked inside the ramshackle structure. Backus sat alone in a chair fast asleep. Stone approached the table, and Backus looked up.

"Got anything to eat?"

"How's about some stew?"

"Sounds fine to me."

Backus arose and walked slowly, with his back bent, to the stove. Stone sat at a table, took off his hat, and reached for his pouch of tobacco. He'd watered and fed the sorrel in the barn before coming inside. Now he could have a leisurely meal and be on his way again.

He lit the cigarette and blew smoke out of the corner of his mouth. Looking around, he noticed a poster on the far wall: $1000 REWARD.

Backus brought a big wooden bowl of beef stew, setting it before Stone. The aroma was delicious, and it was filled with big chunks of meat, potatoes, and carrots. Stone reached for the spoon as Backus walked to the cupboard. He took down a jug and a glass and brought them to Stone.

"No thanks," Stone said. "I don't drink."

Backus ignored him, placing the jug and glass on the table. Then he walked away and sat at the table where he'd been before, and fell asleep again.

Stone spooned up some stew. He expected to return to Clarksdale late that night, and intended to turn his horse over to the sheriff with the hope that somebody would offer a reward for it, since it was stolen. Then he'd see if he could get a refund on his stage fare to Santa Fe, since he had only completed a small leg of the trip.

If he didn't get the reward or a refund, he'd have to find a job until he could earn enough money to buy a horse and travel to Santa Fe on his own. He definitely didn't feel like traveling by stagecoach anymore. Two or three frontier-hardened men on horseback would have the best chance of getting through, but one man could do it too if he was alert and sober.

The main thing is I've got to stay sober, Stone said, chewing beef stew and gazing at the jug of whiskey in front of him. *It's too easy to die out here.*

He finished the meal and pushed the plate away. "How much I owe you?" he asked Backus.

The old man raised himself slowly from his torpor, and told Stone the amount. Stone paid him, wheeled, and walked to the door. The reward poster caught his eye, and he stopped to read it. He took off his hat and scratched his head. "I'll be a son of a bitch," he said, and read the poster again.

"That feller the owlhoots kidnapped was here just t'other night," Backus told him. "I don't remember him exactly, but he was on that stagecoach what got robbed. Sure wish I knew where he was now. Could use me that one thousand smackeroonies."

Stone could use them too. He walked out to the sorrel, tightened the cinch strap, climbed into the saddle, and rode off.

He rolled a cigarette and was pleased with himself for refusing the whiskey inside the hut. *I can beat liquor*. He lit the cigarette, and the saddle creaked underneath him as the sorrel walked toward Clarksdale.

It was night, and Ewell sat at a table in the corner of The Blind Pig in Clarksdale, so-called because it was small, dark, and grungy, full of the scummiest whores on the frontier.

They were mostly old, half-undressed, drunk, and nasty. One of them approached Ewell, her face covered with a thick layer of makeup. She sat beside him and reached between his legs.

"How're you doin', cowboy!" she roared.

He grabbed her wrist. "Leave me alone."

She looked into his eyes and moved away. He took another sip of whiskey, oblivious to the men and women squirming against each other all around him in the tiny room.

If he wanted to go to San Francisco with Rebecca, all he had to do was walk into Sheriff Butler's office and spill his guts out.

But he couldn't betray Beau, his own brother. Frowning, he drained his glass of whiskey. The room was full of tobacco smoke, and he coughed. *Shit*, thought Ewell, *why does life have to tempt a man*?

He thought of Rebecca, and the things they'd done together in the bathtub, and then on the floor like wild animals. He could have her as his very own, if he had that thousand dollars.

But he couldn't betray Beau. Ewell felt as if his brain were being pulled apart. A waitress in a short skirt filled his whiskey glass, and he paid her. He drank the glass, remembering Rebecca.

The pleasure was far more intense with her than any other whore. Somehow they were made for each other. Maybe it was because they were the same age.

She'd been expensive, for the whole afternoon. Now he only had fifty dollars left. He'd been drinking for a while and was drunk.

He looked around and it was as though he and the others were boiling in a cauldron. A woman laughed, and a man sat down at the piano and sang a song.

Ewell wished he could betray Beau. Then everything would be easy. He certainly was mad at Beau. Lately, Beau had never been nice to him, or spent much time with him. Beau always treated him like something contagious that had crawled out from underneath a rock.

Beau always had been too busy for him, running with Ashley and John Stone to parties, hunting deer. Beau never had realized how much Ewell idolized his big brother.

It was terrible to love your brother, and have him show contempt for you. Sometimes when Ewell thought about it, it made him crazy. He touched his hand to his face, and it still hurt from where Beau had slapped him.

His face turned red and he ground his teeth as he recalled Beau slapping him in front of the others. It had hurt his face and head, but more than that it damaged something deep inside him.

It had been humiliating. The men picked on him enough as it was. Beau never had shown Ewell much warmth, even when Ewell had been a little boy.

Well, maybe there'd been a few times Beau had been nice. Ewell remembered being little, and Beau swinging him up onto his shoulders and taking him for a ride, Beau pretending he was the horse. He saw Beau's smiling face in the sunlight of the South, of their childhood together, Beau teaching him to shoot and ride. Ewell heard his father's voice: *Your family comes before anything else in this world—always remember that, Ewell. The bond of a brother to a brother is something no one can break.*

Ewell remembered the time he stole his mother's brooch, and Beau found out about it, but Beau covered for him. No, Beau hadn't always been mean, but he'd been mean most of the time.

Ewell felt like an ugly loathsome beast, because that's the way Beau and everybody else in his family usually had treated him, except for his mother. She protected and loved him, and sometimes let him sleep with her in her bedroom when he was frightened.

Ewell looked around, and nobody was paying any attention to him. That's the way he wanted to be, just another face in the crowd.

There was only one thing Beau respected, and that was courage. Ewell wished he could stand up to Beau, but he couldn't. Ewell wasn't fast with a gun or skillful at fist fighting. He hated pain and avoided it whenever he could. Beau didn't respect a man who wouldn't fight back.

Ewell knew he'd never be a man until he stood up to Beau and made Beau respect him.

The figures whirled around in his brain: Beau, Rebecca, his father and mother, John Stone, Ashley Tredegar, round and round like a roulette wheel in San Francisco, with the little black ball spinning over its circular path, round and round, looking for its place on the wheel of chance.

He wished Beau would walk in the door, sit down with him, and place his arm around his shoulders, but Beau would never do that. Beau considered him a weasel. Beau probably was glad he was gone.

Ewell drank another whiskey. His head was spinning and he felt nauseous. Getting to his feet, he lurched toward the door, pushing his way through sweaty, smelly bodies.

He ran into the nearest alley and vomited. Then he walked a few feet away and sat down, lighting a cigarette.

Beau's ruined my life, Ewell thought, puffing the cigarette. *He oughtta pay for what he done to me.*

Sheriff Butler walked down the main street of Clarksdale, puffing a thin cheroot. He wore his wide-brimmed hat and long riding coat, and the silver bristles of his mustache gleamed in the light emanating from saloons.

Saloons, thought Sheriff Butler, *are more goddamn trouble than they're worth. Still, a man's got to drink. These cowboys come in here lookin' for somethin'—what else they gonna do? They sure as hell give me a pain in the ass.*

Sheriff Butler was known to knock back a few when the occasion allowed. A quiet room, a nice little whore on his lap, yes, Sheriff Butler could appreciate the finer things of life as much as the next man. But there are all those little problems to spoil a man's afternoon and foul up his evening, like somebody shooting somebody else between the eyes, or somebody shoving a knife into somebody's ribs, or a couple of drunken cowboys stringing up a Chinaman to a tree.

It was messy and time-consuming. Many times Sheriff Butler thought about going back to being just a cowboy.

Men nodded to him, and some touched their forefingers to the brims of their hats as he passed. Nobody wanted to tangle with Sheriff Butler. He had a reputation for shooting first and asking questions later.

He came to his office and stepped inside. Deputy Dorsey sat behind his desk, and a young man with curly black hair smoked a cigarette on a bench underneath a print of the flag of Texas.

"This feller wants to talk with you," Deputy Dorsey said to Sheriff Butler.

Sheriff Butler turned to the young man, who appeared to be around sixteen or seventeen. "What's on yer mind?"

"Want to talk with you alone."

"Like to step outside?"

"Rather stay here."

Sheriff Butler scratched his mustache. Many a tough case had been broken by someone stepping forward with special information.

"Deputy Dorsey—check the saloons."

Deputy Dorsey put on his hat and went outside, closing the door behind him. Sheriff Butler pulled his hat lower over his eyes and drew up a chair near the young man.

"What's yer name?" Sheriff Butler asked.

"You ain't gotta know my name," the youth replied. "I'm applyin' for that thousand-dollar reward. I know where John Stone is."

In the lee of a hogback, Stone made his second camp for the night.

His first camp had been a few miles away, but as soon as it got dark he broke camp and slipped away, to make it hard for Indians to locate him.

He spread out his bedroll beneath a rocky ledge and lay down, using his saddle for a pillow. His horse was picketed nearby, and Stone had built no fire.

He'd fallen behind schedule by staying off trails. His main objective was to arrive in Clarksdale alive.

Rattlesnake Canyon seemed far away, like a bad dream. Now he was back to his normal life. He was on his way to Texas again, and nothing would stop him now.

Sheriff Butler crossed the lobby of the Carrington Hotel, his spurs jangling with every step. He climbed the stairs to the second floor and walked down the hall, knocking on a door.

There was no answer. He knocked again, and heard heavy footsteps on the other side of the door.

"Who's there?" asked Edward McManus cautiously.

"Sheriff Butler. I've got news."

The door opened and Edward McManus stood there wearing a green silk robe, a small silver-plated derringer in his hand.

Sheriff Butler entered the room, and it was dark. McManus lit a lamp, and Sheriff Butler saw the large suite with a bed, some chairs, and a table.

A tousled blond head arose from underneath the covers and looked at Sheriff Butler, Maureen McManus, gazing boldly at the law officer. He averted his eyes and sat down. McManus poured him a drink.

Sheriff Butler looked at the spacious and luxurious hotel suite, and compared it with his room at the edge of town. *Rich fellers like McManus get the rooms like this, and blondes like that one makin' eyes at me from under the covers. By Christ, I'd like to tackle her in a jail cell some night. Show her what this tin star is made of.*

The look Maureen McManus beamed back said she was ready for a little night of solitary confinement, if he could find a way. Then Sheriff Butler turned to McManus, and McManus's expression said: *Try it, you son of a bitch, and Clarksdale will have a new sheriff, because bankers pull more weight in small frontier towns than sheriffs with tin badges, and don't you forget it. I'll buy your job any day of the week.*

Sheriff Butler cleared his throat and returned to the business at hand. "Git out yer moneybags, McManus," he said. "We just located John Stone."

Ewell entered the parlor of the Crystal Palace, and Eulalie Parker, the madam, walked up to him. "What can I do fer you, cowboy?"

"Wanna see Rebecca."

"She's busy right now, singin' in the choir. Have a seat—she'll be down in a little while. Care for somethin' to drink?"

"Whiskey."

Ewell sat on a chair and rolled a cigarette with trembling hands. He didn't feel so good, and nobody had given him any money yet. The sheriff told him he'd get it once they had John Stone in custody.

He looked around the parlor, and it was full of men drinking and talking with whores. Some couples walked up the staircase and other couples came down. Ewell lit the cigarette. A black maid brought him a glass of whiskey on a tray.

Ewell felt frightened, and wished he hadn't gone to the sheriff. Something terrible was going to happen and there was no way to stop it. He'd thought he'd be able to get the money and leave right away for San Francisco, but the sheriff told him he'd have to hang around for a while and he only had forty dollars left.

Clarksdale didn't feel safe. Beau's men often came to town. Ewell had to find someplace to hide until the money was paid.

He thought he should ride back to Rattlesnake Canyon and warn Beau, but Beau would kill him, or damn near. Ewell felt a deep, frightening emptiness inside him. He hadn't slept the previous night and had a terrible headache.

All the bad things happen to me, he thought. *I'm the one whose life's a mess. There's other people like John Stone, who ride tall in the saddle, or like Beau, who lead men. How come I'm not one of them? How is it I'm the one who turns them in?* A muffled cry came into Ewell's throat, and he thought: *Just put the thirty pieces of silver in my hand.*

"Wanna come upstairs?" Rebecca asked.

He looked at her, and she stood in front of him with her hands on her hips and the tops of her breasts bursting out the tight bodice of her dress.

"Sit down," he said, motioning to the chair beside him. "I want to tell you something."

"I don't have much time for talk, Ewell," she drawled. "This is the busiest time of my night. I'm here to make money, y'know."

"I'm gittin' the thousand dollars."

The haughty expression on her face changed into that of a greedy little girl. She sat beside him on the sofa. "You really are?"

"Tomorrow or the next day."

"You're sure, or you're just sayin' it?"

"Pretty sure."

"You get that one thousand dollars, Ewell, and I'll go to San Francisco with you or anywhere else you want. I'll be yer woman in every way, you hear?"

He nodded.

"I gotta git back to work now. Don't forget to tell me just as soon as you git the money, all right?"

"You can't talk with me a little while longer?"

"I got to work, honey. I ain't doin' this for fun, you know. You're the only person who can save me, Ewell. You just get that money, and we're gonna be long gone from here."

She patted him on the head as if he were a little dog, kissed his cheek, and a whole new feeling broke over him. *That's right,* he thought, *a woman says yes, everything's fine, you did good, even when you did something the men don't like. Yes, the world of women—that's the world for me, women and whiskey and good times. It's the only world I want to live in.*

"Got to get back to work," she said, and arose, sashaying across the room, sitting next to a man in a long frock coat, putting her arms around his shoulders.

Ewell didn't want to watch. He stood and walked toward the door, passing a whore sitting on a cowboy's lap, and the cowboy was planting a big wet kiss on her cheek.

Ewell stepped outside, and the cool evening air hit him. He thought of Beau and Rebecca, and felt confused again; he wanted to escape from his mind and there was only one way to do it. He looked for the nearest saloon, and one was across the street. He dragged his feet toward it and tried to forget, while the big cowboy moon shone down on him and said: *All is forgotten, I've seen this a thousand times before.* But somehow that big moon seemed red with blood, to Ewell Talbott.

The Earl of Dunwich and Lady Diane Farlington sat at a table in the Emerald City Saloon and looked at the map spread out before them.

"I think we should go to gold-mining country," she said. "I'd like to see the pure naked greed on men's faces as they claw at the ground with their bare hands."

"I'd prefer Indian country myself," Lord Dunwich replied. "I want to sit down and have a reasonable discussion with a savage, and find out how he thinks and what his life is like.

You can do that in some towns, I'm told."

They drank whiskey and examined the map. Dunwich smoked a stogie that burned his throat, and Diane was attired in a cowboy outfit, her wide-brimmed hat on the back of her head.

"May we join you?"

They looked up and saw Sheriff Butler and Edward Mc-Manus.

"By all means sit down," Dunwich said, "Any news?"

Sheriff Butler and McManus sat opposite them on the round table.

"We know where John Stone is, or at least we think we do," Sheriff Butler said.

Diane's heart leapt. "Where?"

"A canyon about ten hours hard ride from here. Stone was taken by the outlaws because one of them evidently knew him during the war. The galoot who told me is a member of the gang. He wants that one thousand dollars real bad."

"He'll get it," McManus said, "if his information is correct."

"It'll take," the Sheriff said, "a posse of about a hundred men to capture those outlaws. I think I can have everybody rounded up by morning."

"May I come?" asked Dunwich.

Sheriff Butler smiled indulgently. "There'll probably be shootin', your worship."

Dunwich pulled out his gun. "I'm armed—it's all right."

"People sure to get killed."

"I'll take my chances."

"It's up to you." Sheriff Butler nodded to Diane, then got to his feet. "I've got a lot of ridin' to do between now and tomorrow mornin'."

He walked toward the door, past tables crowded with raucous cowboys.

Dunwich pulled out his watch. "Won't get much sleep tonight, I guess. Might as well stay up till that posse rides off in the morning."

"We've been lucky so far," Diane said. "Don't press your luck. You don't want to wake up after ten hours of hard riding to a bullet in the brain."

"It'll make a better story that way." Dunwich turned to McManus. "Do you think you'll be coming along with the posse?"

"I leave that kind of activity to younger men."

"Strange," mused Lady Diane, "I wonder why John Stone's old war friend would've abducted him?"

"Who knows what grudges they might be hanging on to?" McManus replied. "The frontier is full of ex-soldiers. Most of the men you meet of Stone's age have been in the war."

"Wish I could've been here for that show," Dunwich said. "What side were you on, Mr. McManus?"

McManus fingered his cigar and smiled. "My own side."

In a seedy unpainted hotel near the saloon district, Ewell Talbott lay on his narrow cot, trying to fall asleep.

He hadn't slept the night before, had been drinking all day, and was sick to his stomach. He'd tried to get drunk, to obliterate the confusion and pain he felt, but the drunker he got, the worse the pain became.

It was like a drill boring through his brain, and he couldn't stop it. If he fell asleep, it'd go away, but he couldn't fall asleep. He chewed his lower lip until it bled.

He'd betrayed Beau, his big brother, the idol of his life. Beau had been everything Ewell wanted to be, and Ewell had sold him down the river.

The posse would shoot to kill, and those they didn't kill, they'd hang.

Ewell thought of Beau swinging from the end of a noose, and bit his lower lip. He wondered what'd happen to poor Veronica. The others could be strung up by their toes, for all Ewell cared, but not Beau, and not Veronica.

It had been so wonderful long ago before the war. Ewell often liked to conjure up the old days, but Beau always was there, and now whenever he thought of Beau he felt crazy.

He tried to think about San Francisco, the tall-masted ships in the harbor and the big wild gambling saloons where fortunes were made and lost every hour.

His back itched; he'd been bitten by a bedbug. He scratched and rolled over, and his thoughts turned to Rebecca, so beautiful, soft, so wild in bed. Everything about her exhilarated him. He'd do anything for her.

He imagined her lying beside him, reaching out for him, but then her face slowly transmogrified, the lines deepened around her mouth, and she became his own mother gazing at him with utter contempt.

Ewell screamed in horror and buried his face in his pillow.

Edward McManus walked down the hotel corridor to his room, his big stomach like a fort in front of him. He inserted the key into the lock, and opened the door.

It was silent in his suite, and a shaft of moonlight landed on the closet door. He looked toward the bed and saw the sleeping form of his wife.

Removing his frock coat, he walked toward the closet. He opened the door and was hanging his coat up when he saw something peculiar in back of the closet. He reached into his pants pocket and whipped out his derringer.

"Come out of there," he said.

The man came out of the closet. He was naked, about McManus's height but much slimmer and younger. McManus recognized him in the moonlight. It was Curly, one of the cowboys who'd rescued them after the stagecoach holdup.

"Light the lamp, would you, Maureen?"

She got out of bed, and she was naked too. She put on her robe, then lit the lamp. The room became suffused with a golden glow.

She looked at him defiantly. Curly appeared sheepish, embarrassed and frightened. The derringer was pointed directly at his groin.

"Put on your clothes and get out," McManus said calmly.

Curly dragged his clothes from underneath the bed and dressed himself as McManus glanced at Maureen's sullen features. Finally Curly was dressed, holding his cowboy hat in his hand. He and Maureen exchanged a quick nervous look.

"Start walking," McManus said, aiming his derringer at Curly, "and if I ever see you again, I'll have your nuts for a saddlehorn."

Curly loped toward the door, opened it, and was gone. McManus locked the door, pushed his derringer into his belt, and turned to Maureen. "Let's have a drink, shall we?"

He poured two whiskeys at the bar and gave her one of the glasses. Then he sat on a chair and lit a cigar.

"Let's understand each other," he said, looking at her calmly. "You satisfy certain of my bodily needs, and I find you entertaining, but there are thousands like you and I can have a replacement in a day. All I've ever asked from you is loyalty, which you may not be able to provide, but anyway, I'm willing to overlook this little episode, because everybody makes mistakes. If it happens again, however, I'll throw you out on your ass."

She stood next to the bed and crossed her arms. "Let me tell you something," she replied. "Maybe I satisfy some of yer body needs, and maybe I might be entertaining to you, but you don't satisfy none of my body needs, and you shore as hell don't entertain me. You kin start a-lookin' for my replacement right now, because, honey, I'm headin' for the rodeo."

He watched as she walked to the closet, pulled down a suitcase, lay it on the bed, and commenced packing.

"Maureen, you'll wind up in a whorehouse."

She ignored him as she stuffed in the clothes, then carried another suitcase from the closet.

"Let's talk this over," he said. "We've been together for a long time."

"Ain't nothin' to talk about."

She walked to the closet, picked out a dress, and took off her robe. She put on clean underclothes, then dropped the dress over her head.

"It's a cruel world out there," he said softly. "Maybe you've forgotten."

"It's cruel wherever you go," she said, sitting in front of the mirror, brushing her luxuriant golden hair. "All I know is I ain't gittin' somethin' I need, and I'm a-gonna git it one way or t'other."

"Maybe you'd better think it over a little more thoroughly, Maureen. You're not getting any younger. If you walk out of this room, I guarantee you that the next room you're in won't be nearly so nice."

"It ain't the room, but *who's* in the room, Edward."

He blew cigar smoke out of his mouth. It wasn't as easy as he'd thought. She wanted a young stud, not an old burping bull with a potbelly.

"Maybe you should wait until morning," he said. "It's not safe out there for a young woman."

"Don't you worry none about me." She put on her bonnet in front of the mirror, then walked to the door. "I'll get the desk clerk to carry my things downstairs."

"I'll carry them for you."

"You might strain yourself, Edward. You know them pains you get whenever you lift things."

She left the room, and he poured himself another drink. A rich man has many things to console him, but still, he'd miss the little bitch.

She returned with the desk clerk, who lifted the suitcases, carrying them out the door. Maureen turned to her husband. "Well," she said, "I guess this is it, Edward. Thanks for everythin'. It was fun for a while."

"Let me give you some money."

He reached into his pocket and took out a handful of gold coins, dropping them into her palm. "I hope you'll be all right, Maureen."

She poured the coins into her purse. "Find somebody yer own age, Edward. You'll be better off."

She winked, turned around, and walked out of the door. McManus stared at the corridor for a few moments, then returned to his chair and sipped his whiskey thoughtfully.

8

IT WAS THE hour before dawn, and a crowd of horsemen gathered in front of the sheriff's office.

They were ranchers, cowboys, businessmen, freighters, farmers, and drifters. Their saddlebags were filled with food; bedrolls were tied to their saddles. Each had guns, rifles, and plenty of ammunition. They were ready for war if that's what it'd take to rid their territory of outlaws.

Dunwich was among them, wearing his British suit with a cowboy hat, and he'd bought a Sharps .50 caliber buffalo gun from a drunken hunter at an exorbitant price. He also had a gunbelt with two holsters and two heavy guns.

In his saddlebags were three pounds of cheese, numerous tins of meat, and two loaves of bread. He had two canteens of water and one canteen filled with the finest whiskey he could buy at that time of night. The atmosphere in the street reminded him of a Saturday morning hunt in the English countryside, except this time they were hunting men who were heavily armed too.

The door opened, and Sheriff Butler stepped onto the planked sidewalk. He wore a gun in a holster and carried a rifle in his right hand.

Looking at the men gathered before him, and they numbered more than a hundred, he said: "From now on, until I release you from duty, you're *lawmen* under my supervision! We're goin' after a bunch of men who're dangerous, so foller my

149

orders and don't try nothin' on yer own! If any of you has any doubts about what we're gonna do, this is the time to turn around and go home. I don't want any man here who might choke if we find ourselves shootin'!"

He paused, and the riders milled around in the street. No one left the posse.

"Who's got the dynamite?" Sheriff Butler asked.

A hand went up in the posse. "I do!"

"You ride near me. The rest of you fall in behind us."

Sheriff Butler climbed onto his horse and put the spurs to its flanks. The horse trotted out of town, and the posse followed, hoofbeats thundering in the streets and echoing off buildings, as they headed for Rattlesnake Canyon.

Stone rode into Clarksdale at noon and brought his horse to a stop in front of the sheriff's office. He climbed down from the saddle, threw the reins over the rail, and went inside.

A deputy sat behind the desk, reading a newspaper.

"Sheriff in?" Stone asked.

"Nope."

"When you expect him?"

"A few days."

"Got a problem," Stone said. "That horse I'm ridin' is stolen, but I don't know who it's stolen from, and I didn't steal it myself."

The deputy lay the newspaper on the desk. "How did you come by it?"

"Somebody gave it to me."

"Who?"

"I didn't get his name?"

"Where do you know him from?"

"He held up a stagecoach I was on a few days ago east of Deadman's Flats."

The deputy wrinkled his forehead. "What's yer name?"

"John Stone."

The deputy touched his fingers to his stubbled jaw. "That name sounds familiar."

"Somebody's offering a thousand dollars for me."

The truth dawned on the deputy. "John Stone! Is *that* who you are? How'd you git loose?"

"The outlaws let me go."

"Somebody's already claimed the reward money. The posse left for Rattlesnake Canyon at dawn, to bring you back."

"Who claimed the reward money?"

"A kid, about sixteen I'd say. Clean-cut, with black curly hair. Acted kinda peculiar. You all right, mister?"

Stone left the sheriff's office and headed straight for the nearest saloon. He felt entitled to at least one drink, because he hadn't had a drop since leaving Rattlesnake Canyon.

The bartender poured him a glass, and Stone drank it down. He nodded to the bartender to pour another.

Stone thought about Ewell and Beau. Ewell always had been an odd little person, withdrawn and quiet, with strange mannerisms. Beau had been ashamed of Ewell.

Stone wanted to warn Beau, but the posse had too long a head start. Beau'd have a fight on his hands when Sheriff Butler and his men arrived.

Stone thought of poor lost Veronica. What would happen to her? How odd that his life intersected again with hers and Beau's just before a major catastrophe struck them again.

Stone realized he was on his fourth glass of whiskey. He finished it and walked out of the saloon, heading for the stagecoach office.

He walked down the sidewalk, stomach in and chest out, feeling fairly healthy for a change. It'd been good to sleep under the stars, far from the suffocating atmosphere of Rattlesnake Canyon, and San Antonio was straight ahead. All he needed was more money.

He entered the stagecoach office. A man wearing a green visor stood behind the cage, writing something. "What can I do for you?" he asked pleasantly.

"I was on the stagecoach to Santa Fe a few days ago," Stone explained, "and I was taken prisoner by some outlaws not far from Deadman's Flats. I just got back in town, and I was wondering if I could get a refund on my trip."

"Afraid not," the man said. "Pitkin Overland went out of business two days ago."

Stone thought of Pitkin and his girlfriend on the top floor of the King Hotel in Denver. "You know what happened to Raymond Slipchuck, the Pitkin driver?"

"Last thing I heard he was drinkin' at The Blind Pig."

• • •

Stone entered The Blind Pig, and it was like a pure vision of hell. A man in a greasy shirt played a piano badly, and the air was thick with smoke. Couples squeezed and squirmed in the booths, and Slade, the cowboy from the earlier stagecoach ride, sat by himself with his back to a wall, facing the door. Slade and Stone looked at each other, and although they'd sat together inside the cramped stagecoach all the way from Arizona, they didn't say a word or even acknowledge each other's existence. Stone wondered what Slade's game was, as he penetrated more deeply into the murky depths of The Blind Pig.

A middle-aged woman wearing smeared cosmetics slithered up to Stone. "You wan' make very fine love?" she asked with a smile.

"I'm looking for an old stagecoach driver named Ray Slipchuck."

"He ees asleep. I fuck heem teel he can't move. You make love with me, yes?"

She brushed her lips against his jaw, and touched her breasts to his shirt.

"Let the old man sleep," she said, looking up into his eyes. "You and me—we go back to the room, hokay?"

"Where is he?"

She pointed, and he walked toward the far corner. Sprawled against the wall, his eyes closed, was Slipchuck.

Stone sat next to him. Slipchuck's hat lay on the floor, and Stone bent over to pick it up. Slipchuck had long gray hair, hadn't shaved for several days, and smelled awful. A waitress walked by with a bottle and a tray of glasses. Stone raised his finger in the air.

"One whiskey," he said.

Slipchuck opened his eyes and groaned.

"Make that two whiskeys."

She poured the drinks, and Stone paid. Slipchuck put his hat on and stared at Stone.

"Where the hell did you blow in from?"

"Just got in town about a half hour ago."

"Thought you'd be dead by now. What happened?"

"Had a vacation for a few days. Heard you lost your job."

"Pitkin spent the family jewels," Slipchuck said, "and I'm flat on my ass again."

"You'll find something else."

"Nobody wants to hire an old man."

"You can drive a stagecoach as well as anybody I ever saw."

"What did them outlaws do with you?"

"We drank a lot."

"Wish they'd kidnapped me. There's a thousand-dollar reward for you. Maybe you can git it?"

"You know who put up the money?"

"McManus and an Englishman, and the Englishman was in the posse with the rest of 'em. I been ridin' in posses before most of 'em was born, but that hardass sheriff said I was too old for this one, and they wouldn't let me go with 'em, the no-good bastards. I hope they get their asses shot off."

Stone and Slipchuck drank all afternoon, and Slipchuck passed out about five o'clock. Stone carried Slipchuck to the broken-down hotel where he was staying, and dropped him into bed.

Then Stone returned to the street. He was drunk again and disgusted with himself for letting it go so far. He walked heavily down the planked sidewalk, a cigarette dangling out the corner of his mouth, and saw the Carrington Arms. Veering across the street, he was nearly run down by a wagon.

"Watch whar you're goin'—you goddamn drunk!"

Stone walked into the lobby of the Carrington Hotel and approached the clerk at the front desk. "Is Edward McManus in?"

The clerk told him the room number. Stone climbed the stairs, walked down the hall, knocked on the door. There was no response. He knocked again. Still nothing. As he was turning to walk away, he heard footsteps inside the room. The door opened and McManus stood there, bleary-eyed, his collar button undone.

Stone entered the room. One empty bottle and one half full sat on the coffee table.

McManus collapsed onto a chair. "She left me for another man," he said plaintively.

Stone reached for the bottle and filled up McManus's glass, then filled a glass for himself. "A man who was one of my best friends probably will be killed tonight."

"I never realized how much I loved her."

"He's gone rotten, and I guess he deserves whatever happens to him, but he was a good friend when I was young."

They drank whiskey and talked drunkenly. The bed was unmade and the curtains were half-closed.

"Thought of killing myself," McManus said. "But the thought soon passed."

"His brother turned him in," Stone muttered.

McManus looked at Stone. "Talk to her for me. Tell her how much I need her."

"You can't convince a woman of something unless she wants to be convinced."

"Don't know why I love her, because she's stupid, indolent, narrow-minded, and coarse."

"Your wife is a beautiful woman."

McManus wheezed. "Maybe that's why I need her. I love beauty." McManus's huge belly hung out of his shirt like a wrinkled pink watermelon.

"I wanted to thank you for posting the reward money."

"Was the only decent thing to do. Wait a minute! How come you're here so soon?"

"Outlaws turned me loose. Guess they got sick of me."

"Doesn't look as if they harmed you much. Why'd they take you away?"

"Needed a hostage, I guess."

"I think I'll kill myself," McManus said. "I can't go on like this."

"Have another whiskey," Stone suggested.

They continued to drink, grumble, and complain. McManus passed out two hours later. When Stone realized McManus wasn't responding to him anymore, he arose from his chair and pitched toward the door.

He left the hotel and crossed the street, heading for the Emerald City. It was going to be a night of hard drinking, there was no question about it. He walked inside, bought a drink at the bar, and carried it to a table in the corner. *I'll sip this one slowly,* he said to himself.

He brought the whiskey to his lips and thought again of Beau. The posse would come to Rattlesnake Canyon soon. They'd attack in the darkness and shoot every outlaw they saw.

Stone wondered if there was another way out of the canyon. An able commander would have paths of retreat planned in advance for every contingency, and Beau had been an able commander.

"I knew I'd find you here."

Stone looked up and saw Lady Diane Farlington, a worried expression on her face. She sat next to Stone. "Heard you were released by the outlaws. You know about Paul? He's gone on the posse, and I'm afraid he'll be killed."

"It's a possibility," Stone admitted.

"You're drunk. Do you have a place to stay?"

"Not yet."

"Paul's bed is empty. You can have it if you like."

"I'm not ready to go to sleep yet."

"Don't you think you've had enough?"

"Leave me alone."

"I won't leave you alone. We made an arrangement. You're supposed to tell me about your life. When are you going to start?"

"How much money are we talking about."

"Twenty dollars for two days of your time, and we'll pay expenses."

"Tell you what," Stone said. "You give me enough to buy a horse and saddle, and I'll tell you anything you want, as long as you don't use my real name."

"How much is a horse and saddle?"

"Fifty dollars."

"Will you tell me about the Apaches?"

"I'll tell you anything you want to know."

"And the war?"

"Whatever you want."

She took out her notepad. "We might as well begin now."

He leaned back in his chair and wondered where to start. *What's a man's life? Where does the thread begin? I followed a crooked path to nowhere. I killed men in battle. I've slept under the stars. I had a good friend . . .*

He drank some whiskey and began to ramble about the war. He told her stories he'd heard around campfires, and described a few unusual things that happened to him. He told her truth and lies, like any man.

Whiskey sloshed down his throat, and he talked about his

five years on the frontier. When he couldn't remember specific details he improvised. He knew she wanted good stories and gave them to her.

"What about the Apaches?" she asked.

He didn't want to reveal the truth about his friend Lobo, because it would be painful to recall, so he made up a series of wild adventures off the top of his head. She wrote furiously, and he seemed to grow larger in her eyes.

She'd never met anybody like him. What a life he'd led. What a man he was.

But then she caught herself. His eyes were rolling around in his head as he gesticulated with his big arms, describing an incident that may or may not've really happened. *Is he just another saloon hero?*

Mike Holtzman, the black-bearded cowboy from Deadman's Flats, staggered into the Crystal Palace. He'd just spent his last quarter at a saloon across the street and was hoping to find somebody he knew, some old waddie pal from one of the big trail drives, to buy him a drink or two, maybe even three.

He pushed his hat to the back of his head and placed his hands on his hips, gazing across the room. A sea of heads stretched before him, but no one was familiar.

His eyes swept back over the room, and in the corner near the front window, at a small round table, sat the woman he'd seen a few days before, the one who dressed like a man.

Holtzman's eye moved to the right, and his eyes fell on John Stone.

Holtzman remembered him, and drew his gun.

At the table, Stone was talking about the time some people tried to lynch him in Texas, when he became aware of a terrific commotion. Men hollered and ran toward the walls and doors. Stone got to his feet and reached for his guns. Diane screamed and raised her fists to her cheeks. Holtzman rushed forward and opened fire, and Stone's hat flew off his head. Stone triggered both his Colts and Holtzman fanned the hammer of his Starr Model 1863. The room echoed with the sound of guns, and smoke billowed in the light of the oil lamps.

Holtzman stopped firing. He stood loosely, a quizzical expression on his face, then dropped his gun. Stumbling, his legs went numb and he fell to the floor.

Stone holstered his gun, and turned to Diane, his face a

cold furious mask. The stories he'd been telling and what just happened were mixed together, flying around in his head, and he said, "Put that in your notes—did you get it all down?"

The pen had fallen from her hand. She couldn't speak. The expression on her face reminded him of Veronica.

He grabbed her hand. "Let's get out of here."

He pulled her to her feet and made his way to the door, passing patrons and waitresses lying under tables and kneeling behind the bar. He dragged her behind him, and she had difficulty moving her feet; they were mildly paralyzed.

They passed through the doors and came to the sidewalk. She looked up into his eyes. He'd been like a great drunken beast, and now he'd awakened.

His heart beat like a drum in his chest. He'd gone from complete repose to a fight to the death in a matter of seconds, and the adrenaline had hit his heart like nitroglycerine. He breathed deeply through his nostrils and was ready for anything.

The street was empty. He saw the sign for the Carrington Hotel and decided it was the best place to go. Wrapping his arm around her waist, he half carried her to the hotel. They went up to her room, and she unlocked the door.

It was a suite similar to the McManus suite, except that it had two beds, each pushed against an opposite wall.

She lit the lamp on the dresser. "I need a drink," she said, and walked to the bar. "Want one?"

"No."

"Are you sure?"

"I'm sure."

He sat on a chair and rolled a cigarette. She poured herself a stiff shot of whiskey and sat on a chair opposite him, crossing her legs. Taking off her hat, she threw it across the room.

"I think I'm going back to England," she said. "Enough is enough."

He lit the cigarette and drew smoke into his lungs. The alcohol reasserted itself, and he felt tired. He sprawled in the chair and his eyes drooped. "I'm going to stop drinking," he said. "If you ever see me taking a drink again, remind me of what I just said." He bent over and took off his boots. "Which bed is Dunwich's?"

"That one."

Stone moved toward it and dropped his hat onto the bedpost.

Then he unstrapped his guns. He hung the holsters on another bedpost, pulled out a gun, and dropped onto the bed, getting comfortable, closing his eyes.

She stared at the gun in his hand. "Aren't you afraid that thing might go off while you're asleep?"

"Hasn't yet."

"You're not going to take off your clothes?"

"Too tired."

He rolled over and she finished her glass of whiskey, blew out the lamp, and walked to her bed. Undressing, she climbed underneath the covers. She closed her eyes and saw the man with the black beard lying dead on the floor of the Crystal Palace.

9

STONE HEARD A door open behind him and woke up suddenly. He spun around on the bed and brought up his Colt.

"Don't shoot," said Dunwich. "Once is enough."

Dunwich walked into the suite, his coat off and a bandage around his left shoulder. He was pale and looked ten years older. Dropping into a chair, he saw the bottle and poured himself a drink with his good hand.

"Everything went fine at first," he said, "and then the outlaws started firing back. I got hit, and so did a few of the others, but finally we wiped them out."

"You wiped *all* of them out?" Stone asked.

"Maybe a few got away—it'd be hard to say. They didn't have much of a chance against us. We had them outnumbered."

"What about the women and children?"

"We brought them back with us. They're in jail."

Stone got out of bed and pulled on his boots. He strapped on his gunbelts and tied the holsters to his legs.

"Where are you going?" Diane asked.

"To see those people."

Stone put on his hat and walked out of the room. He left the hotel and saw a huge crowd gathered down the street in front of the sheriff's office.

He made his way toward them, anxious about Beau and Veronica. A large number of horses were tied in the street, and dead men hung head down over saddles. Stone looked at the first dead man, whose head was flecked with dried blood, and recognized one of the outlaws from Rattlesnake Canyon.

He checked the other bodies, his anxiety mounting, and recognized many of the other outlaws, but not Beau, Cavanaugh, Shattuck, or Chance Stevens. He saw a deputy standing nearby, evidently the guard, and walked up to him.

"This all of them?" he asked.

"All we got."

Stone entered the sheriff's office, and it was crowded with townspeople and posse members congratulating one another. Stone spotted Sheriff Butler.

"I wonder if I could see the women and children," Stone said.

"Who're you?" asked Sheriff Butler.

"John Stone."

Sheriff Butler smiled faintly. "So you're John Stone. Pleased to meet you. Got some money for you, by the way. The owner claimed that horse you brought in, and left you forty dollars for yer trouble."

Sheriff Butler opened his desk, took out a strongbox, opened it with a key, and handed Stone an envelope containing the money.

"Can I see the women and children?"

"Foller me."

Sheriff Butler unlocked the door that led to the cell block area. Stone walked into the passageway between two rows of three cells each, filled with women and children from Beau's gang.

Gloria and Veronica weren't among them, but he recognized some of the others. There were five women and eight children, and all looked scared.

"What's going to happen to them?" Stone asked.

"They'll stay here until the state finds something to do with them."

"Have you charged them with any crimes?"

"Don't know what to charge them with. Have to wait until the judge comes to town."

"You can't keep them locked up if they haven't been charged, can you?"

"Who says I can't?"

"The law."

Sheriff Butler touched his thumb to his chest. "I'm the law around here."

Stone looked at the woman nearest him. "Do you have any money?"

She didn't reply. Stone reached into his shirt and handed her the white envelope. "Here's something to tide you over."

She looked at him scornfully. "We wouldn't be here right now, if it wasn't for you."

"I'm not the one who betrayed you."

She ignored the envelope and turned away from him, and so did the others. Stone stood uneasily for a few moments, his face becoming red, and then turned and walked out of the cell block, heading for the Carrington Hotel.

In another part of town, Edward McManus and Deputy Dorsey climbed the steps of a cheap hotel made so crudely that light could be seen through the cracks in the planked walls. It was dark and smelled of urine and whiskey.

They made their way down the corridor, and Deputy Dorsey stopped in front of a door. He knocked and then they waited, listening to an argument between a man and a woman in the room across the way.

The door opened, and they saw a young man with black hair. "You got the money?" he asked.

McManus nodded and held up the valise. Ewell opened the door wider. "Come on in."

They entered the tiny room, and it contained only a bed and a small dirty window. Ewell closed the door, and the room smelled of vomit.

McManus opened the valise and upended it on the bed; the bag of money fell out. Ewell opened the bag and looked inside.

"It's all there," McManus said.

McManus and the deputy left the room. Ewell sat on the bed and emptied the bag of coins onto it. He dipped both his hands into the coins and lifted them into the air, letting the coins fall through his fingers. He'd always wanted to have a lot of money, and there it was. Now he had to get out of town.

He divided the money into both sides of his saddlebags, threw them over his shoulder, and left his hotel room, heading for the Crystal Palace.

• • •

Stone entered the hotel suite. Dunwich lay on his bed, propped up on a pillow, drinking whiskey out of his flask.

"I gave you your stories," Stone said. "Now give me my money. I've got to leave town."

"We're leaving too," replied Dunwich, "but I don't trust the stagecoaches anymore. Maybe our ambassador in Washington can convince your government to give us a cavalry escort. I'll wire him as soon as I recover my strength."

"I don't have much time," Stone said. "If I stay in Clarksdale much longer, it might not be good for my health. Some of those outlaws got away, and I think they're looking for me. Evidently they think I'm the one who betrayed them."

Dunwich sat up in his bed. "Diane, hand me my wallet."

She picked it up off the dresser, gave it to him, and he counted out the money, passing it to John Stone.

Stone and Diane looked at each other with a knowledge of something that could've been, but never will be, and both knew it. Their paths were parting, and it was a big country out there.

Stone took her hand. "It's not likely we'll ever meet again," he said.

"Please don't say that," she replied.

"Well, maybe around some other campfire someday."

"Yes, that's how it'll be."

He turned to Dunwich. "Good-bye. It's been interesting."

"Yes, hasn't it? If you're ever in Gloucestershire, look me up. I can promise no one will shoot at you."

Stone looked at him. "No one can make that promise, not on this earth."

"Yes," said Dunwich, "I suppose you're right."

He and Diane watched as the tall ex-soldier shouldered his saddlebags and walked from the room.

"Interesting character, eh?" said Dunwich.

It cost Diane something to keep from running after Stone, to say the things to him that she'd never said to anyone else. *Get hold of yourself*, she thought as she sat by the window. *It just won't do*. The curtains blew at the window where she sat, the air of the strange wild country rolling over her, and she felt the spirit of John Stone. She breathed it deeply into herself, and that's what she'd take back with her to England.

• • •

Ewell walked into the Crystal Palace and looked for Rebecca.

"I know who you want," the madam said to him, "but she's at prayer right now. Could I interest you in Caroline?"

The madam pushed a hard-looking young woman forward, but Ewell shook his head.

"Just want Rebecca."

"You'll have to wait. Can I get you a whiskey?"

Ewell sat on a chair in the corner where he'd be out of the way, drew the saddlebags between his legs, and looked at the afternoon array of whores. There were only a few of them, and a few cowboys. The atmosphere was subdued, compared to the frolic at night. The drapes were pulled back partially, and long spears of sunlight streamed through the gloom.

Ewell knew John Stone was in town, and also knew members of his old gang escaped the posse. He wanted to get out of Clarksdale as soon as possible.

He rolled a cigarette, sat hunched over his chair, and wished Rebecca would hurry up, because it wasn't safe for him to be up and about. *They're all alike,* he thought. *Why the hell am I waiting for Rebecca anyway? Why don't I just grab one of these other whores and run away with her? They all want to go to San Francisco with a man who's got a thousand dollars. I've got a thousand dollars—goddammit—why do I have to sit around and wait?*

But then, being a quiet, meek sort of person, he waited. Then he began hearing things. Every footstep in the whorehouse made him jump. A woman's laughter in an upstairs room sent a chill through him. It sounded like Veronica for a moment. Is that where Veronica wound up, in some crazy whorehouse? *What have I done?*

He was scared, jumpy, and depressed, and wished he hadn't opened his big mouth, but it was too late now. He had to go through with his original plan, because he had nothing else. With luck, he'd be in San Francisco in a week or two.

He spotted Rebecca walking down the staircase with a man who looked like a cowboy or maybe a freighter. She patted the man on the shoulder, curtsied, then headed for Ewell.

"You got the money?" she asked.

"It's right here." He tugged the saddlebags.

"I don't believe you."

"Look for yerself."

She sat beside him, picked up the saddlebags, and looked inside casually. She saw gold coins, and her eyes lit up.

"It's a thousand dollars," he said. "Will you leave with me now?"

She pushed her long fingernails into the pile of coins. "You're damn right I will, Ewell. You kept yer part of the bargain, and I'll keep mine. You take this money to yer room and stay there. I'll be with you as soon as I can git there, and we'll figger out what to do, but you just remember that yer my man now, Ewell, and I'll do anythin' you say."

The stable was at the edge of town, and it was an old rickety barn leaning perilously to one side. Stone needed to buy a good cheap horse, and had been told he might be able to get a bargain at this out-of-the-way stable.

He entered through the big square doorway, and the stable was dark and quiet. Horses were lined in the stalls, flicking their tails and stomping their hooves. Looking up, Stone saw cracks in the roof that admitted narrow splinters of light.

"Anybody here!" he asked.

There was no answer. Stone saw something move behind a bale of hay, and pulled out his guns, jumping behind the side of a stall.

Stone was motionless for a few moments, and nothing happened. Maybe it was one of the rats that lived in the stable, or maybe he'd imagined it. A horse stared at him with that quiet uncanny knowledge that horses have in their eyes.

He holstered his guns and stood up. "Hello—anybody here!"

Again there was no answer. Maybe the stable manager was out back. He walked in that direction, then saw a sign that said OFFICE on a door at the top of some stairs.

He climbed the stairs, and they creaked underneath the worn soles of his boots. The window in the office was dark, and a bird flew among the rafters of the barn. The fragrance of hay and horse manure was heavy in the air.

Stone came to the door of the office, and knocked. There was no answer. He reached to the doorknob, turned it, and opened the door. Directly in front of his eyes were the twin barrels of a shotgun.

"What you want, varmint?"

"I want to buy a horse."

"What you sneakin' around for?"

"I think an old friend of mine might try to kill me."

"Happens all the time," the man said, and he stepped out of the shadows.

He was short, slim, and had long white hair and a long white mustache and beard. The front brim of his dirty cowboy hat was pinned to the crown.

"I'll show you the horses."

They went downstairs, and Stone looked them over while the stable manager extolled the virtues of each. Stone wished he had time to ride a few before he made up his mind, but didn't have time. He had to get out of town.

He selected a chestnut gelding with good lines. "How much for this one?"

"That there horse is named Tomahawk. He can turn on a quarter an' give back fifteen cents change."

The haggling began. Stone didn't have much money, and had to save every dollar he could. The stable manager fought for every penny. It went on for five minutes, then Stone gave up and paid the asking price.

Next they haggled over a saddle. Again Stone ended up paying the asking price.

He saddled the horse, tightened the cinch, and threw his saddlebags behind the saddle.

"Happy trails," said the stable manager.

Stone rode into the sunlight, and it momentarily blinded him. He looked around, saw blue shadows on his eyeballs, fading to reveal nobody hiding behind a barrel pointing a rifle at him.

Tomahawk seemed glad to be out of the barn. He pranced and snorted, shaking his black snout.

Stone rode out of town and headed east toward Texas. He wanted to travel until midnight, to put as much distance as possible between him and anyone who might be pursuing him.

Tomahawk moved into the open sage, and Stone sat tall in the saddle, while back in Clarksdale a man in a black shirt stood against the wall in an alley at the edge of town and watched him.

• • •

Ewell lay on his bed, smoking a cigarette, and there was a knock on his door. He sat up quickly, pulled his gun, and pointed it at the door.

"Who's there?"

"Rebecca!"

He holstered his gun and rushed to the door, opening it up. She stood there in a red dress, a bonnet covering her head. "Darling," she said.

They embraced; their lips touched.

"I'm so glad you got here," he said, nuzzling his nose in her fragrant throat.

"Where's the money?"

"In the saddlebags underneath the bed."

"Oh, I'm so happy," she said. "Kiss me, darling."

They embraced again, and his back was to the open door. Their lips touched and tongues entwined. She was passionate and thrilling in his arms, and he thought to himself: *It was worth it*.

He heard the soft fall of a footsteps behind him, and perked up his ears. Something sharp and incredibly awful cut his spinal cord suddenly. Ewell gurgled and fell to the floor.

Slade stood over Ewell, the bloody blade in his hand. "Get the money," he said to Rebecca.

In a quick movement he closed the door and affixed the latch. She pulled the saddlebags from underneath the bed and laid them on the covers. Opening the flaps, she found the coins.

"It's all here," she said.

Slade slashed Ewell's jugular, then wiped the blade on Ewell's pants.

"Let's get out of here," he said, picking up the saddlebags.

They left the room and closed the door behind them, leaving Ewell in the widening pool of blood on the floor.

10

STONE OPENED HIS eyes. He was lying on his side in a small clearing amid cottonwood trees, and it was morning. The sun shone and birds twittered above him.

He rolled over and saw Beau seated on the ground beside him, pointing a gun at his head.

"Morning," Beau said. "Don't go for your guns, if you want to live awhile longer."

Stone thought it might be a bad dream. He shook his head, but Beau was there, wearing his black shirt with the buttons down the sides, and his wide-brimmed black hat.

"Guess you know I've got to kill you, Johnny."

Stone slowly brought himself to a sitting position opposite Beau, whose gun was pointed directly at Stone's head. Beau hadn't shaved for a while, and his face looked more shadowy and sinister than usual. Stone couldn't see Beau's horse. Beau must have picketed it far away, and then crept up on Stone like a snake in the grass.

"How'd you find me?" Stone asked.

"Saw you in Clarksdale, but you didn't see me."

"I didn't turn you in," Stone said. "I know that's what you think, but it wasn't me."

"Don't be despicable."

"It was Ewell."

"Just when I think you can't get any lower, you take another step down."

"Where's Cavanaugh and the others?"

"We'll meet by the Pecos in ten days, but first there's a duty I must discharge." He closed one eye and sighted down the barrel on John Stone's head.

"Could I have one last cigarette?"

"You don't deserve it."

There was silence for a few moments. Stone gazed into Beau's eyes.

"Okay," Beau said. "One last cigarette—for old times' sake."

Stone took out his bag of tobacco and slowly rolled. "Where's Veronica?"

"We got her out."

"Gloria?"

"You betrayed us all, and now you're worried about what happened to the women? Did you think the sheriff would give a tea party when he paid his call?"

"Beau," Stone said, "I didn't betray you. I'm not made that way. You and Ashley were the closest friends I ever had, but even if you were a stranger, I wouldn't betray you. Money isn't that important to me."

"You're a good talker," Beau said, "but you're not good enough."

Stone puffed his cigarette. He thought about trying a quick draw and a roll-out, but Beau had his sights trained on him and would blow him away before he moved two inches.

"Ewell did it, and I can prove it," Stone said.

"Don't stoop to that, Johnny."

"Many people in Clarksdale know who sold you out. I can give you their names. It's probably common knowledge by now."

"Ewell'd never betray me. He's a son of the South, but you're not. You're practically a Yankee, the way you talk."

Stone stared at him and said, "I think you know Ewell betrayed you, but it sticks in your craw. So you blame it on me, because you don't like my politics these days."

"I think you've had enough of that cigarette, Johnny. Say your prayers."

Stone looked at the big black barrel of the gun, and a chill passed over him. "You're not going to shoot me in cold blood."

"I'm executing you herewith for the betrayal of my trust, and for the destruction of my command."

"Beau—wake up—this is me—John Stone! We grew up together, for Christ's sake! You can't just shoot me as if I were an animal!"

"Say your prayers, Johnny. You've come to the end of your road."

"Why don't we let Mr. Colt decide it?"

Beau hesitated. Stone realized he'd hit a soft spot.

"Let's make it gladiatorial," Stone continued, earnestly pressing his advantage. "Trial by combat, like in medieval times. If I'm the man you say I am, I'll be killed, and if you're wrong about everything, you'll be killed. Come on, Beau—you and I've been through a lot together. You can't just shoot me in cold blood. You've got to give me a sporting chance."

Beau smiled bitterly. "You son of a bitch."

"Gentlemen settle their differences in duels. They don't gun each other down like this. Let Mr. Colt have his say."

Their eyes met, and it was like flint and steel. Beau thought for a few minutes, his gun still leveled at Stone's head. "All right, Johnny," he said at last. "Your point is well taken. Get up slowly, and don't try anything strange, because I'm looking for an excuse to kill you and you know it."

"I'll be real slow, Beau."

Stone arose carefully, using no sudden movements, and pulled himself to his full height, stretching out his arms.

Beau got up, his gun still aimed at Stone. They were about ten feet apart. Beau eased the hammer on his gun forward, and lowered the gun into his holster.

"Are you ready?" he asked.

"Why don't you just walk away, Beau. There's still time to stop this thing."

"That's what I'd expect you to say, Johnny. You always want the easy way out, but you see—there is no easy way out. Mr. Colt has to decide it. That's what you said, and that's the way we're going to play it."

"What do you think Ashley would want you to do, Beau?"

"Ashley's dead, and you'll be with him soon."

"Beau, I'm going to tell you something. There's no way you can beat me. When we had that shoot-out a few days ago, I let you win, because I didn't want to hurt your feelings. Let me be very clear about this, Beau—if you draw on me, you're a dead man."

Stone looked at Beau and saw a man with one lung who didn't have much time anyway. *If I get killed in this*, Beau's eyes seemed to be saying, *you'd be doing me a favor.* Then an expression of indescribable hatred came over Beau's face, and he went for his gun.

Stone slapped his hand down, whipped out his Colt, and fired. The sound of the shot echoed over the sage, and the tip of Beau's barrel wasn't even out of his holster.

The bullet rocked Beau, and his hat fell off. A second later a dark stain appeared on Beau's black shirt. Beau looked as if he were becoming unstrung. He tried to raise his gun for another shot, and Stone fired again.

Stone saw the friend of his youth drop to his knees, blood spouting over the front of the shirt. Beau dropped his gun and raised the palms of his hands to his chest as he looked at Stone.

" . . . in the other world . . ."

Beau pitched forward onto his face and lay still. Stone stared at him for a few moments, then holstered his gun and kneeled beside Beau, rolling him onto his back.

Beau's eyes were closed, and particles of sand were mixed with the blood dribbling out of his nostrils. Underneath the gore, he looked at peace.

Stone leaned forward and placed his hand on Beau's black hair. "May the Lord have mercy on your soul."

Stone felt delirious as he took out his bag of tobacco and rolled a cigarette. Looking up at the sky, he wondered when the vultures would notice the fresh meat. *I've got to bury him.*

He didn't have a shovel, but maybe he could dig a hole with his tin plate.

He removed the tin plate from his saddlebags and got down on his knees, scooping dirt out of the ground. It was hard work, and soon he had to take his shirt off. Then he continued hacking at the ground.

It took two hours to gouge a shallow grave out of the thick-packed earth. Stone picked up Beau and laid him gently in the grave, crossing Beau's arms over his chest. Then he stood at the edge of the grave and bowed his head.

"Lord," he said, "I commend my friend Beauregard Talbott into your hands. He was a good soldier, a good friend, and he always did his duty as he saw it, no matter what the odds. We had differences, and that's why he's lying down there, but that doesn't mean he wasn't a good man.

"I know he did bad things, but he thought they were proper, so judge him on his intentions, as well as the results. And remember, oh Lord, that we don't ask to come into this world, and we have to make the best of what we find here. It's not that easy sometimes. Take that into consideration too."

Stone wasn't accustomed to praying and couldn't think of anything else to say. He wished he could remember an appropriate psalm.

"Well, at least he died with his boots on," Stone muttered as he reached down and picked up the tin plate.

He threw dirt on Beau, and soon Beau couldn't be seen anymore. It formed a mound over him, and Stone covered the mound with rocks. Then he cut branches off a cottonwood tree, made a cross, and tied it with string. He placed the cross atop the grave and set to work breaking camp.

There wasn't much to do. All he had was Tomahawk, his saddlebags, blanket, and the clothes on his back. He lashed the blanket and saddlebags behind the saddle, and placed his foot in the stirrup, raising himself up.

He wheeled Tomahawk around and faced Beau's grave. Sitting erectly in the saddle, his old cavalry hat slanted over his eyes, he raised his arm slowly in a West Point regulation salute, snapped it out, and pulled Tomahawk east toward San Antone.

GILES TIPPETTE

Author of the best-selling WILSON YOUNG SERIES, BAD
NEWS, and CROSS FIRE is back with his most exciting
Western adventure yet!

JAILBREAK

Time is running out for Justa Williams, owner of the Half-
Moon Ranch in West Texas. His brother Norris is being
held in a Mexican jail, and neither bribes nor threats can
free him.

Now, with the help of a dozen kill-crazy Mexican *banditos*,
Justa aims to blast Norris out. But the worst is yet to come:
a hundred-mile chase across the Mexican desert with fifty
federales in hot pursuit.

The odds of reaching the Texas border are a million to nothing . . . and if the Williams brothers don't watch their backs,
the road to freedom could turn into the road to hell!

JAILBREAK
by
Giles Tippette

On sale now, wherever Jove Books are sold!

**Turn the page for a sample of
this exciting new Western.**

AT SUPPER NORRIS, my middle brother, said, "I think we got some trouble on that five thousand acres down on the border near Laredo."

He said it serious, which is the way Norris generally says everything. I quit wrestling with the steak Buttercup, our cook, had turned into rawhide and said, "What are you talking about? How could we have trouble on land lying idle?"

He said, "I got word from town this afternoon that a telegram had come in from a friend of ours down there. He says we got some kind of squatters taking up residence on the place."

My youngest brother, Ben, put his fork down and said, incredulously, "*That* five thousand acres? Hell, it ain't nothing but rocks and cactus and sand. Why in hell would anyone want to squat on that worthless piece of nothing?"

Norris just shook his head. "I don't know. But that's what the telegram said. Came from Jack Cole. And if anyone ought to know what's going on down there it would be him."

I thought about it and it didn't make a bit of sense. I was Justa Williams, and my family, my two brothers and myself and our father, Howard, occupied a considerable ranch called the Half-Moon down along the Gulf of Mexico in Matagorda County, Texas. It was some of the best grazing land in the state and we had one of the best herds of purebred and cross-bred cattle in that part of the country. In short we were pretty well-to-do.

But that didn't make us any the less ready to be stolen from, if indeed that was the case. The five thousand acres Norris had been talking about had come to us through a trade our father had made some years before. We'd never made any use of the land mainly because, as Ben had said, it was pretty worthless, because it was a good two hundred miles from our ranch headquarters. On a few occasions we'd bought cattle in Mexico and then used the acreage to hold small groups on while we made up a herd. But other than that, it lay mainly forgotten.

I frowned. "Norris, this doesn't make a damn bit of sense. Right after supper send a man into Blessing with a return wire for Jack asking him if he's certain. What the hell kind of squatting could anybody be doing on that land?"

Ben said, "Maybe they're raisin' watermelons." He laughed.

I said, "They could raise melons, but there damn sure wouldn't be no water in them."

Norris said, "Well, it bears looking into." He got up, throwing his napkin on the table. "I'll go write out that telegram."

I watched him go, dressed, as always, in his town clothes. Norris was the businessman in the family. He'd been sent down to the University at Austin and had got considerable learning about the ins and outs of banking and land deals and all the other parts of our business that didn't directly involve the ranch. At the age of twenty-nine I'd been the boss of the operation a good deal longer than I cared to think about. It had been thrust upon me by our father when I wasn't much more than twenty. He'd said he'd wanted me to take over while he was still strong enough to help me out of my mistakes and I reckoned that was partly true. But it had just seemed that after our mother had died the life had sort of gone out of him. He'd been one of the earliest settlers, taking up the land not long after Texas had become a republic in 1845. I figured all the years of fighting Indians and then Yankees and scalawags and carpetbaggers and cattle thieves had taken their toll on him. Then a few years back he'd been nicked in the lungs by a bullet that should never have been allowed to heed his way and it had thrown an extra strain on his heart. He was pushing seventy and he still had plenty of head on his shoulders, but mostly all he did now was sit around in his rocking chair and stare out over the cattle and land business he'd built. Not to say that

I didn't go to him for advice when the occasion demanded. I did, and mostly I took it.

Buttercup came in just then and sat down at the end of the table with a cup of coffee. He was near as old as Dad and almost completely worthless. But he'd been one of the first hands that Dad had hired and he'd been kept on even after he couldn't sit a horse anymore. The problem was he'd elected himself cook, and that was the sorriest day our family had ever seen. There were two Mexican women hired to cook for the twelve riders we kept full time, but Buttercup insisted on cooking for the family.

Mainly, I think, because he thought he was one of the family. A notion we could never completely dissuade him from.

So he sat there, about two days of stubble on his face, looking as scrawny as a pecked-out rooster, sweat running down his face, his apron a mess. He said, wiping his forearm across his forehead, "Boy, it shore be hot in there. You boys shore better be glad you ain't got no business takes you in that kitchen."

Ben said, in a loud mutter, "I wish you didn't either."

Ben, at twenty-five, was easily the best man with a horse or a gun that I had ever seen. His only drawback was that he was hotheaded and he tended to act first and think later. That ain't a real good combination for someone that could go on the prod as fast as Ben. When I had argued with Dad about taking over as boss, suggesting instead that Norris, with his education, was a much better choice, Dad had simply said, "Yes, in some ways. But he can't handle Ben. You can. You can handle Norris, too. But none of them can handle you."

Well, that hadn't been exactly true. If Dad had wished it I would have taken orders from Norris even though he was two years younger than me. But the logic in Dad's line of thinking had been that the Half-Moon and our cattle business was the lodestone of all our businesses and only I could run that. He had been right. In the past I'd imported purebred Whiteface and Hereford cattle from up North, bred them to our native Longhorns and produced cattle that would bring twice as much at market as the horse-killing, all-bone, all-wild Longhorns. My neighbors had laughed at me at first, claiming those square little purebreds would never make it in our Texas heat. But they'd been wrong and, one by one, they'd followed the example of the Half-Moon.

Buttercup was setting up to take off on another one of his long-winded harrangues about how it had been in the "old days" so I quickly got up, excusing myself, and went into the big office we used for sitting around in as well as a place of business. Norris was at the desk composing his telegram so I poured myself out a whiskey and sat down. I didn't want to hear about any trouble over some worthless five thousand acres of borderland. In fact I didn't want to hear about any troubles of any kind. I was just two weeks short of getting married, married to a lady I'd been courting off and on for five years, and I was mighty anxious that nothing come up to interfere with our plans. Her name was Nora Parker and her daddy owned and run the general mercantile in our nearest town, Blessing. I'd almost lost her once before to a Kansas City drummer. She'd finally gotten tired of waiting on me, waiting until the ranch didn't occupy all my time, and almost run off with a smooth-talking Kansas City drummer that called on her daddy in the harness trade. But she'd come to her senses in time and got off the train in Texarkana and returned home.

But even then it had been a close thing. I, along with my men and brothers and help from some of our neighbors, had been involved with stopping a huge herd of illegal cattle being driven up from Mexico from crossing our range and infecting our cattle with tick fever which could have wiped us all out. I tell you it had been a bloody business. We'd lost four good men and had to kill at least a half dozen on the other side. Fact of the business was I'd come about as close as I ever had to getting killed myself, and that was going some for the sort of rough-and-tumble life I'd led.

Nora had almost quit me over it, saying she just couldn't take the uncertainty. But in the end, she'd stuck by me. That had been the year before, 1896, and I'd convinced her that civilized law was coming to the country, but until it did, we that had been there before might have to take things into our own hands from time to time.

She'd seen that and had understood. I loved her and she loved me and that was enough to overcome any of the troubles we were still likely to encounter from day to day.

So I was giving Norris a pretty sour look as he finished his telegram and sent for a hired hand to ride it into Blessing, seven miles away. I said, "Norris, let's don't make a big fuss about this. That land ain't even crossed my mind in at least a couple of years. Likely we got a few Mexican families squatting down there and trying to scratch out a few acres of corn."

Norris gave me his businessman's look. He said, "It's our land, Justa. And if we allow anyone to squat on it for long enough or put up a fence they can lay claim. That's the law. My job is to see that we protect what we have, not give it away."

I sipped at my whiskey and studied Norris. In his town clothes he didn't look very impressive. He'd inherited more from our mother than from Dad so he was not as wide shouldered and slim-hipped as Ben and me. But I knew him to be a good, strong, dependable man in any kind of fight. Of course he wasn't that good with a gun, but then Ben and I weren't all that good with books like he was. But I said, just to jolly him a bit, "Norris, I do believe you are running to suet. I may have to put you out with Ben working the horse herd and work a little of that fat off you."

Naturally it got his goat. Norris had always envied Ben and me a little. I was just over six foot and weigh right around one hundred and ninety. I had inherited my daddy's big hands and big shoulders. Ben was almost a copy of me except he was about a size smaller. Norris said, "I weigh the same as I have for the last five years. If it's any of your business."

I said, as if I was being serious, "Must be them sack suits you wear. What they do, pad them around the middle?"

He said, "Why don't you just go to hell."

After he'd stomped out of the room I got the bottle of whiskey and an extra glass and went down to Dad's room. It had been one of his bad days and he'd taken to bed right after lunch. Strictly speaking he wasn't supposed to have no whiskey, but I watered him down a shot every now and then and it didn't seem to do him no harm.

He was sitting up when I came in the room. I took a moment to fix him a little drink, using some water out of his pitcher, then handed him the glass and sat down in the easy chair by the bed. I told him what Norris had reported and asked what he thought.

He took a sip of his drink and shook his head. "Beats all I ever heard." he said. "I took that land in trade for a bad debt some fifteen, twenty years ago. I reckon I'd of been money ahead if I'd of hung on to the bad debt. That land won't even raise weeds, well as I remember, and Noah was in on the last rain that fell on the place."

We had considerable amounts of land spotted around the state as a result of this kind of trade or that. It was Norris's business to keep up with their management. I was just bringing this to Dad's attention more out of boredom and impatience for my wedding day to arrive than anything else.

I said, "Well, it's a mystery to me. How you feeling?"

He half smiled. "Old." Then he looked into his glass. "And I never liked watered whiskey. Pour me a dollop of the straight stuff in here."

I said, "Now, Howard. You know—"

He cut me off. "If I wanted somebody to argue with I'd send for Buttercup. Now do like I told you."

I did, but I felt guilty about it. He took the slug of whiskey down in one pull. Then he leaned his head back on the pillow and said, "Aaaaah. I don't give a damn what that horse doctor says, ain't nothing makes a man feel as good inside as a shot of the best."

I felt sorry for him laying there. He'd always led just the kind of life he wanted—going where he wanted, doing what he wanted, having what he set out to get. And now he was reduced to being a semi-invalid. But one thing that showed the strength that was still in him was that you *never* heard him complain. He said, "How's the cattle?"

I said, "They're doing all right, but I tell you we could do with a little of Noah's flood right now. All this heat and no rain is curing the grass off way ahead of time. If it doesn't let up we'll be feeding hay by late September, early October. And that will play hell on our supply. Could be we won't have enough to last through the winter. Norris thinks we ought to sell off five hundred head or so, but the market is doing poorly right now. I'd rather chance the weather than take a sure beating by selling off."

He sort of shrugged and closed his eyes. The whiskey was relaxing him. He said, "You're the boss."

"Yeah," I said. "Damn my luck."

I wandered out of the back of the house. Even though it was nearing seven o'clock of the evening it was still good and hot. Off in the distance, about a half a mile away, I could see the outline of the house I was building for Nora and myself. It was going to be a close thing to get it finished by our wedding day. Not having any riders to spare for the project, I'd imported a building contractor from Galveston, sixty miles away. He'd arrived with a half a dozen Mexican laborers and a few skilled masons and they'd set up a little tent city around the place. The contractor had gone back to Galveston to fetch more materials, leaving his Mexicans behind. I walked along idly, hoping he wouldn't forget that the job wasn't done. He had some of my money, but not near what he'd get when he finished the job.

Just then Ray Hays came hurrying across the back lot toward me. Ray was kind of a special case for me. The only problem with that was that he knew it and wasn't a bit above taking advantage of the situation. Once, a few years past, he'd saved my life by going against an evil man that he was working for at the time, an evil man who meant to have my life. In gratitude I'd given Ray a good job at the Half-Moon, letting him work directly under Ben, who was responsible for the horse herd. He was a good, steady man and a good man with a gun. He was also fair company. When he wasn't talking.

He came churning up to me, mopping his brow. He said, "Lordy, boss, it is—"

I said, "Hays, if you say it's hot I'm going to knock you down."

He gave me a look that was a mixture of astonishment and hurt. He said, "Why, whatever for?"

I said, "*Everybody* knows it's hot. Does every son of a bitch you run into have to make mention of the fact?"

His brow furrowed. "Well, I never thought of it that way. I 'spect you are right. Goin' down to look at yore house?"

I shook my head. "No. It makes me nervous to see how far they've got to go. I can't see any way it'll be ready on time."

He said, "Miss Nora ain't gonna like that."

I gave him a look. "I guess you felt forced to say that."

He looked down. "Well, maybe she won't mind."

I said, grimly, "The hell she won't. She'll think I did it a-purpose."

"Aw, she wouldn't."

"Naturally you know so much about it, Hays. Why don't you tell me a few other things about her."

"I was jest tryin' to lift yore spirits, boss."

I said, "You keep trying to lift my spirits and I'll put you on the haying crew."

He looked horrified. No real cowhand wanted any work he couldn't do from the back of his horse. Haying was a hot, hard, sweaty job done either afoot or from a wagon seat. We generally brought in contract Mexican labor to handle ours. But I'd been known in the past to discipline a cowhand by giving him a few days on the hay gang. Hays said, "Boss, now I never meant nothin'. I swear. You know me, my mouth gets to runnin' sometimes. I swear I'm gonna watch it."

I smiled. Hays always made me smile. He was so easily buffaloed. He had it soft at the Half-Moon and he knew it and didn't want to take any chances on losing a good thing.

I lit up a cigarillo and watched dusk settle in over the coastal plains. It wasn't but three miles to Matagorda Bay and it was quiet enough I felt like I could almost hear the waves breaking on the shore. Somewhere in the distance a mama cow bawled for her calf. The spring crop were near about weaned by now, but there were still a few mamas that wouldn't cut the apron strings. I stood there reflecting on how peaceful things had been of late. It suited me just fine. All I wanted was to get my house finished, marry Nora and never handle another gun so long as I lived.

The peace and quiet were short-lived. Within twenty-four hours we'd had a return telegram from Jack Cole. It said:

YOUR LAND OCCUPIED BY TEN TO TWELVE MEN STOP CAN'T BE SURE WHAT THEY'RE DOING BECAUSE THEY RUN STRANGERS OFF STOP APPEAR TO HAVE A GOOD MANY CATTLE GATHERED STOP APPEAR TO BE FENCING STOP ALL I KNOW STOP

I read the telegram twice and then I said, "Why this is crazy as hell! That land wouldn't support fifty head of cattle."

We were all gathered in the big office. Even Dad was there, sitting in his rocking chair. I looked up at him. "What do you make of this, Howard?"

He shook his big, old head of white hair. "Beats the hell out off me, Justa. I can't figure it."

Ben said, "Well, I don't see where it has to be figured. I'll take five men and go down there and run them off. I don't care what they're doing. They ain't got no business on our land."

I said, "Take it easy, Ben. Aside from the fact you don't need to be getting into any more fights this year, I can't spare you or five men. The way this grass is drying up we've got to keep drifting those cattle."

Norris said, "No, Ben is right. We can't have such affairs going on with our property. But we'll handle it within the law. I'll simply take the train down there, hire a good lawyer and have the matter settled by the sheriff. Shouldn't take but a few days."

Well, there wasn't much I could say to that. We couldn't very well let people take advantage of us, but I still hated to be without Norris's services even for a few days. On matters other than the ranch he was the expert, and it didn't seem like there was a day went by that some financial question didn't come up that only he could answer. I said, "Are you sure you can spare yourself for a few days?"

He thought for a moment and then nodded. "I don't see why not. I've just moved most of our available cash into short-term municipal bonds in Galveston. The market is looking all right and everything appears fine at the bank. I can't think of anything that might come up."

I said, "All right. But you just keep this in mind. You are not a gun hand. You are not a fighter. I do not want you going anywhere near those people, whoever they are. You do it legal and let the sheriff handle the eviction. Is that understood?"

He kind of swelled up, resenting the implication that he couldn't handle himself. The biggest trouble I'd had through the years when trouble had come up had been keeping Norris out of it. Why he couldn't just be content to be a wagon load of brains was more than I could understand. He said, "Didn't you just hear me say I intended to go through a lawyer and the sheriff? Didn't I just say that?"

I said, "I wanted to be sure you heard yourself."

He said. "Nothing wrong with my hearing. Nor my approach to this matter. You seem to constantly be taken with the idea that I'm always looking for a fight. I think you've got the wrong brother. I use logic."

"Yeah?" I said. "You remember when that guy kicked you in the balls when they were holding guns on us? And then we chased them twenty miles and finally caught them?"

He looked away. "That has nothing to do with this."

"Yeah?" I said, enjoying myself. "And here's this guy, shot all to hell. And what was it you insisted on doing?"

Ben laughed, but Norris wouldn't say anything.

I said, "Didn't you insist on us standing him up so you could kick him in the balls? Didn't you?"

He sort of growled, "Oh, go to hell."

I said, "I just want to know where the logic was in that."

He said, "Right is right. I was simply paying him back in kind. It was the only thing his kind could understand."

I said, "That's my point. You just don't go down there and go to paying back a bunch of rough hombres in kind. Or any other currency for that matter."

That made him look over at Dad. He said, "Dad, will you make him quit treating me like I was ten years old? He does it on purpose."

But he'd appealed to the wrong man. Dad just threw his hands in the air and said, "Don't come to me with your troubles. I'm just a boarder around here. You get your orders from Justa. You know that."

Of course he didn't like that. Norris had always been a strong hand for the right and wrong of a matter. In fact, he may have been one of the most stubborn men I'd ever met. But he didn't say anything, just gave me a look and muttered something about hoping a mess came up at the bank while I was gone and then see how much boss I was.

But he didn't mean nothing by it. Like most families, we fought amongst ourselves and, like most families, God help the outsider who tried to interfere with one of us.

WESTERNS!

at least a savings of $3.00 each month below the publishers price. Second, there is never any shipping, handling or other hidden charges—Free home delivery. What's more there is no minimum number of books you must buy, you may return any selection for full credit and you can cancel your subscription at any time. A TRUE VALUE!

Mail the coupon below

To start your subscription and receive 2 FREE WESTERNS, fill out the coupon below and mail it today. We'll send your first shipment which includes 2 FREE BOOKS as soon as we receive it.

Mail To: 557-73554
True Value Home Subscription Services, Inc.
P.O. Box 5235
120 Brighton Road
Clifton, New Jersey 07015-5235

YES! I want to start receiving the very best Westerns being published today. Send me my first shipment of 6 Westerns for me to preview FREE for 10 days. If I decide to keep them, I'll pay for just 4 of the books at the low subscriber price of $2.45 each; a total of $9.80 (a $17.70 value). Then each month I'll receive the 6 newest and best Westerns to preview Free for 10 days. If I'm not satisfied I may return them within 10 days and owe nothing. Otherwise I'll be billed at the special low subscriber rate of $2.45 each; a total of $14.70 (at least a $17.70 value) and save $3.00 off the publishers price. There are never any shipping, handling or other hidden charges. I understand I am under no obligation to purchase any number of books and I can cancel my subscription at any time, no questions asked. In any case the 2 FREE books are mine to keep.

Name _____

Address _____ Apt. # _____

City _____ State _____ Zip _____

Telephone # _____

Signature _____
(if under 18 parent or guardian must sign)
Terms and prices subject to change.
Orders subject to acceptance by True Value Home Subscription Services, Inc.